Upon entering the house, he headed straight for his bedroom. His agenda called for listening to Frankie Beverly and Maze until falling out for a nap. After his nap he had planned to take a shower and head for the clubs. He walked through his bedroom on to the bathroom to pay the water bill. He finished and returned to the bedroom. Initially his high had made him blind to the difference in how his room currently looked as opposed to how he had left it that morning. Slowly reality set in. Speaking to himself, he commented, "What the hell happened here?" Gone were the piles of dirty clothes. Gone were the dirty dishes left lying all over the place. The bed had been made with fresh sheets and the clutter had been replaced with order. Worse yet, the room smelled of air freshener and ammonia.

He proceeded straight to Nedra's room, knocked and walked in before receiving an answer and asked, "Hey, you know what happened to my bedroom?"

She smiled like the keeper of the key to a hidden treasure and replied, "Sure I know what happened. What happened is I cleaned it up. Don't thank me."

ROUGH ON RATS
AND
TOUGH ON CATS

CHRIS PARKER

Genesis Press Inc.

Black Coral

An imprint of Genesis Press Inc.
Publishing Company

Genesis Press, Inc.
P.O. Box 101
Columbus, MS 39703

ISBN: 1-58571-154-3
Manufactured in the United States of America

First Edition

Visit us at www.genesis-press.com
or call at 1-888-Indigo-1

DEDICATION

For those who have believed in me as I have in them.

ACKNOWLEDGMENTS

I acknowledge Genesis Press for taking a risk on an unknown, unpublished, and unproven author. Additionally, I graciously, as well as gratefully, acknowledge the contributions of Deatri King Bey, my editor, for the insightful suggestions and feedback. Let's see how it goes.

CHAPTER 1

"Batman!!! Batman!!!! You woke?"

He woke up that Friday morning with a headache out of this world. The culprit? A night of partying combined with acute sleep deprivation. Under penalty of perjury, he would have sworn that while asleep someone had crawled through his ear canal and into his brain with an ice pick. The throbbing in his head was made worse by the outrageous banging at the bedroom door. There was no need in guessing who the tormentor was. His roommate, in her zeal to rouse him, stood outside doing an improvisation of the Miami police during a hostage rescue. His first thought was whether he had returned his stash of reefer to its secret hiding place. Confident he had, he gingerly lifted his head to see what time it was. It took a few seconds for his eyes to adjust to the glowing red light shining from the electronic digital clock radio. After more than a little effort, he was able to decipher the numbers 6, 2, and 0. Subtracting the twenty odd minutes he had advanced the time, he concluded it was around six a.m.

Having appointed herself his guardian angel, Nedra persisted in banging on the door like a wild banshee. Knowing her as he did, he could imagine the glee this provided her. Fighting through the despair, he visualized her on the other side of the door dressed in an oversized T-shirt and pink slippers, braids pulled back and sporting that silly ass Homey the Clown grin she always wore when giving him grief. Exuding all the persona of Queen Latifah, he needn't doubt the hand not used in the assault on his door was planted on her hip in disgust.

Interspersed between knocks, Nedra shouted, "Batman!!! Batman!!!! You woke?"

There was no need of Batman thinking she would go away. It just wasn't in her professional, African-American, female composition to do so. Summoning every bit of strength he could muster, he weakly managed, "Sure Nedra…for Christ's sake, I'm woke. You think you could give that health department routine a rest now?"

With no acknowledgement of his comments, the banging ceased. *Thank God for small miracles*, he thought. Removing the covers and rolling out from the waist, Batman sat upright on the side of the bed. Almost instantly, he began looking for the bottle of generic painkillers he'd purchased the week before from the Haitian dollar store on 79th and Biscayne. He located the bottle among dirty dishes and other clutter on the nightstand next to the bed. In one motion, he leaned over and retrieved them. The white label on the bottle read "Non-Aspirin, Extra Strength Painkillers, 500mg," but could have read, "Poor Man's Tylenol." Bargain basement wasn't just a slogan when it came to the Haitian dollar store. For two dollars and thirty cents, he had managed to walk out with the painkillers, a pack of sinus decongestants, and a bottle of athlete's foot powder. For all he knew he could have been buying sugar pills. Regardless, he popped the top, sprinkled four in his right palm and threw them into the back of his mouth.

Satisfied he had done all he reasonably could short of blowing out my brains to abate the agony, Batman slid into his blue uniform trousers and walked topless into the living room. Nedra was seated at one end of the black leather sofa, deep into the morning news. Rick Sanchez, her favorite anchor, was interviewing a local politician on the effects of the latest court ruling on Elian Gonzales's fight with the INS. Flashing at the bottom of the screen was the caption, "Exclusive Interview." Batman slowed, grudgingly mumble good morning then continued through to the kitchen in search of a glass of OJ to finish washing down the presumptive pain tablets.

Having done so, he returned to the living room and took a seat on the opposite end of the sofa from Nedra. He placed the glass with the juice he had yet to drink on the floor by his feet and gazed in her direction, hoping to convey a less than appreciative look of contempt for her previous bad behavior. No sooner had he found the sweet spot did Rick finish his interview as the newscast gave way to the morning string of commercials. Nedra, not wishing to indulge the advertisers, changed the channel to C-SPAN.

Batman watched as C-SPAN televised a clip of one of his two least favorite uncles: Uncle Clarence Thomas and Uncle Ward Connerly. On this morning, Uncle Clarence stood in a black suit at the head of the class answering questions from students. Batman wondered why anyone would want to hear anything Uncle Clarence had to say. Nedra and he had discussed Thomas's appointment many times over and differed drastically in their opinion of him. She thought Justice Thomas should be applauded for having overcome the obstacles in his life to rise to the position of Supreme Court justice. He, on the other hand, thought Thomas and Connorly were both tomatoes. They had been farm raised and picked by the white conservative system as would a tomato.

In his mind, both Thomas and Connorly had ridden the affirmative action train all the way to their current positions of influence. However, now they were each about the business of dismantling the engine and tearing up the tracks to prevent anyone of their same color or life experiences from realizing their destination. To hear them speak of how they made it to their current positions represented the zenith of hypocrisy. The penalty if they were to change their anti-affirmative action rhetoric was to be discarded, as in the case of a tomato with a spot. Hence, they were no different from tomatoes.

C-SPAN ended its coverage of Justice Thomas, and Nedra turned back to the previous channel. Batman sat quietly with his eyes closed and head tilted back, fighting off the headache. He had hoped that Nedra would have struck up a conversation. This would have afforded him an opportunity with which to weigh in with his request.

Nedra, on the other hand, was quite familiar with his "can you loan a brother a dime" routine. It was obvious he was suffering the effects of a nasty hangover. His normal treatment regimen was to lie on his back with his head hung over the mattress. She sensed his presence meant he wanted more than just to keep her company. Usually, he would have waited until she asked what it was that he wanted.

However, as luck would have it, time was not on his side.

Deciding this was as good a time as any to cut in, Batman commented innocently, "Nedra, I need your car to go to work."

She turned slowly away from the television to give him her full attention. "And what, may I ask, is wrong with the Gator?" she asked with little to no regard for the pain he was in.

The Gator she referred to was his pride and joy. It was also his sole possession and his biggest bill outside of normal living expenses—a black 1998 Lincoln Navigator, complete with tan leather interior, CD changer, gold appointments, and twenty-two inch chrome rims. He had bought it on the cheap through an on-line repossession agency. They had gotten it from an enterprising drug entrepreneur whose business, because of the increasing competition in the market, had taken a turn for the worse. It had taken the bulk of his savings to have the bullet holes in the body fixed and the glass replaced. However, aside from the consequences of its previous use and the fact that it got horrible gas mileage, it was more than a single black bachelor could ask for.

Batman gingerly lifted his head and grimaced. Her body language told him he had his work cut out for him. To avoid stringing it out, he elected to use the Reader's Digest version. "The Gator's down for the count. She's not running right now."

The corner of Nedra's left eye twitched, signaling an eruption was immanent. No doubt irate, she responded, "Batman, don't give me that crap. What do you mean she's not running? She was running last night when you parked her."

"Yeah, but she's not running now."

"O.K., why isn't she running now?"

Smiling weakly, he offered, "She's out of gas, and I don't have money to get any."

Without breaking her stare, Nedra pointed the remote toward the television. The anchor's face blanked out, and the picture tube turned black. This was his signal that the berating was about to begin.

"Batman, hear me and hear me well," she said, rising to stand threateningly over him. "First off, that a man who works forty hours a week doesn't have gas to put in his car is his business. And secondly, there's a hell of a lot of difference between a car that's not running and one that's out of gas."

Batman returned his head to its previous resting position and momentarily closed his eyes. He opened them to see her still bearing down on him with those baby browns that were on their way to becoming red with anger. For him the issue was a simple one. She owned two cars, and he needed one. According to his arithmetic, her honoring his plea would have caused minimal to no material harm to herself. It wasn't as he was asking for first pick. Hell, he would have been more than happy to glad ass around in the hoopdy. Therefore, her position mystified and slightly peeved him.

Seemingly perplexed, he casually responded, "You think so?"

"Yes, I most certainly do."

It was obvious that Nedra had grown weary of debating the matter. For his part, he wasn't getting any kicks out of it either. What started out as a friendly game of tag was headed toward being a brawl.

Defensive, but cautious not to push the envelope to far, he replied, "Well if there's such a big difference, why don't you do this. Take my keys. Give me yours. Go outside and try to crack ole girl. And then come back and let a brotha know just what the difference is."

For her it was time to pull the gloves off. She had become frustrated with their shadow boxing. Attempting to land a right cross, she exhaled slowly. "Batman, if you were my husband, I'd put poison in your orange juice."

Using Winston Churchill's rebuttal, he ducked under her right cross and threw a jab of his own. "Nedra, if you were my wife, I'd drink it."

His quick counter landed flush on the chin and staggered her. Deciding she wasn't in the mood for their usual give and take, Nedra took a step back and replied emphatically, "*No*, Batman, you *can not* use my car. What you can do is have your trifling ass ready in twenty minutes, and I will drop you off at work."

Satisfied she'd gotten him told, she spun around like Cinderella and exited to her bedroom, all the time grumbling about his ineptness.

Batman decided he'd better not mess with her this day and returned to his bedroom to retrieve his orange uniform shirt. To prevent having to search them out, he always attempted to keep three hung on the back of his bedroom door. This allowed him to save time when in a rush, which he usually was. It was then that he noticed the body lying like a dead log in his bed. It had been positioned along side him the entire night, but somehow he had awakened and forgotten it was there. If his memory served him right, he had picked her up from Big Daddy's on the corner of 141st and 7th Ave. Not certain, he reasoned he had gone to only two clubs that night. Big Daddy's was the last, so she had to have come from there.

Being a fair-minded brother, he felt it was important where he picked his dates up. He appreciated the sexual favors sistahs offered and hoped that they were as grateful for the in-kind return. However, some sistahs got up the next morning and thought they were going to be taxied all over Miami—Not! Once he had this dirty-south sistah he agreed to take home. By the time he was through, he had taken her to pick up her food stamps, taken her baby to daycare, taken her little sistah to put some money on the books for her baby's daddy at the Stockade, and her brother out to South Florida Detention to meet with his probation officer. Hell, the detention center was way down in the Everglades. He didn't consider himself a hard-core brother, but once burned, he set limits.

All the same, he thought back to Nedra waiting to drop him off and realized it was of little consequence where he got her from since he wouldn't be returning her. He approached the bed and looked over at her to see just how well he had done. As is often the case, guys meet females and take them home for the extended party favors thinking they've snagged a star. The drinks and weed along with them having fixed themselves up for the night makes them look much better than they often turn out to look the next morning. Although he was generally not choosy, he did have standards. The problem was, they were strictly interpreted but loosely enforced.

That said, he liked women of all shades and sizes. What was most important to him was that they kept themselves as best they could. He, as anyone, would be lying to say he didn't have preferences. It was just that his preferences weren't such that he couldn't objectively dismiss them if the situation dictated.

For instance, size. He preferred an eight to a twelve, but could go as low as a six or as high as a sixteen—again, circumstances dictating. Shade, on the other hand, depended on his mood for the evening. Being versatile, he could move from being a fine fella for that high yellow…. to being quite all right if she were black as midnight.

Satisfied his date fell within an acceptable range for his morning after taste, he shook her gently but firmly. "Hey, wakeup. I gotta go to work."

Unresponsive, she laid as if dead. This left him no choice but to take it to level two. He took hold of the covers and viciously snatched them off her. She squirmed butt-naked on the mattress then rolled over with a look of total bewilderment.

My Lord, he thought, *I may need to lower that morning after rating after all.*

Besides her, in between where she and he had slept, lay a blond wig and red silk panties. He'd noticed since being in Miami that it was common for sistahs to wear wigs to clubs. The smoke got in their hair and was a headache to get out. However, two days earlier, his bed had received its once a week making, and he had not noticed either. As such, he assumed these were hers.

Without waiting for her to come fully to her senses and doing his best to imitate his cartoon namesake, he whispered loudly, "Hi, I'm Batman." *Oh well, he thought, sometimes I can be too silly for my own good.* She didn't stir.

"Look, I'm sorry to have to wake you, but I got to get to work. You think you could grab your stuff? I'm running way late."

From the look on her face, he could tell it was all coming back.

She'd be hard pressed to testify to the specifics, but the generalities she was definitely aware of. Sistah calls her girlfriend. Sistah and girlfriend go to club. Sistah leaves with guy she just met. Sistah goes to guy's crib and gets to know him on a more personal level. Guy wakes up in the morning and asks sistah to leave. Yeah, from the look he could safely say she was depending more on the generalities than the specifics.

Half awake, she murmured, "Sure. Sure. Just let me use the restroom."

With the aid of a little coaxing, she rose slowly to an upright position, grabbed her underwear and clothes then stumbled into the restroom. From his position in the bedroom, he heard her plop down on the toilet and start the water in the basin.

"Could you get me a towel?" she shouted out to him.

"There's one in the sink," he answered, aware he was running out of time.

After a moment, she shouted back, "How about a drying towel?"

He stood and walked to the bathroom door. Their eyes met. "Well I normally dry off with the face towel. What do you need a drying towel for?"

Sounding insulted, she responded, "I want to take a shower."

Batman raised his voice to interject a tone of urgency. He moved to the sink, turned the water off and quickly replied, "Look, I'd love for you to take a shower. Better yet, I'd like to take one with you. But I'm running late for work, and I have to get out of here, pronto."

As could be expected, she was not at all happy with the response. Regardless, she rose and walked back into the bedroom. The stretch marks around her midsection told him he was dealing with somebody's baby's mama. The pouch suggested it might even be two somebody's baby's mama. She looked hesitantly at him as though she wanted to speak. Thinking it better not said, she turned and went back into the bathroom to dress.

He was in no mood for a morning after conversation and elected to return to the living room. Fully dressed for work, he looked in on Nedra who had reoccupied her usual spot on the sofa. As he had before, he took a seat on the opposite end.

"Ready when you are, Boo," he said, happy the worse seemed over.

Obviously aggrieved, she turned and stared at him. "Batman, you can't be ready," she said, turning up her nose. "Damn!!! You smell like sex and reefer. Just because you work on the back of a damn garbage truck, don't mean you have to act like you have no sense. You may go to work like that, but you're not riding anywhere in my car smelling like that."

"What do you mean I smell like sex and dope," he replied, miffed at all the changes she was putting him through just to get a freaking ride. "It's not like I work in an office. You just said it yourself. I work on the back of a garbage truck."

Nedra couldn't pass on an opportunity to get him told. "Just because you work in filth doesn't mean you have to be filthy. You're not going anywhere with me smelling like a herd of billy goats."

She held her wrist toward his face and pointed her index finger at her watch. "You have exactly nine minutes forty-three seconds and counting to wash your ass and be ready or else you'll have to find another way to work."

Batman knew she was serious. Without further debate, he shot into the bedroom and on to the bathroom. Seeing his date was dressed and ready, he quickly commented, "Look, take a seat. I'm just going to take a duck shower. I'm going to duck in and duck out."

It took two minutes for him to wet his body, soak down, rinse off, dry off with the face towel, put on deodorant, and spray on a mist of cologne. Satisfied he could pass Nedra's smell test, he summoned his friend, saying, "Let's go."

Exasperated, he returned to the living room. "Alright, Boo, ready when you are."

Nedra absolutely hated him calling her "Boo," or any other pet names. She thought it was ghetto, which she did everything in her power to disassociate herself from. He was surprised she didn't say something stupid. Rather than take it up as an issue, she instead took one look at his friend and asked, "Where's she going?"

Batman had hoped Nedra would go along without making a scene. Normally, she would bite her tongue then rip him later. However, on this morning she seemed resolute to get an argument kicked off.

Attempting to deflect the tone of her comment, he said innocently, "Oh, I was going to get you to drop her off around the block."

Nedra switched to her soul sistah routine. "Damn you, Batman, hear me well. I don't mind taxing you," she stopped in mid-sentence to consider her words. "I take that back. I do mind, but against my better judgment, I do it anyway. But I'm not about to taxi your friends around Miami. Besides, she smells like sex and weed, and ain't nobody getting in my car smelling like that."

Before he had a chance to reply, Nedra raised her hand to quiet him. "Look, Negro, I'm not going to debate or argue with you. I'm going to the car. You have exactly two minutes before your ride leaves." Nedra walked out to the car and left them standing in the living room.

His friend, fully insulted, didn't know what to make of Nedra's comments. She had never met Nedra and didn't know whether she was psychopathic or not. He could tell she was really pissed. She had wanted to respond in the bedroom but had thought better. However, he knew sistahs, and knew this was the last straw.

Clearly anxious, he turned to her and said, "Look, here's two dollars, you think you could get home? The bus stop is just two blocks away."

"Do I think I can get home?" she asked rhetorically as if she hadn't heard correctly. "I don't know who you think I am, but I ain't some project whore. It took all I had not to put your little friend in her place. She's lucky I don't like shit this early in the morning or else it would be on. Look, give me those two dollars," she said, snatching it from his hands, "and let me get out of here before I go postal. I knew better than to deal with a sorry ass like you anyway."

Batman knew she was right to be upset and felt bad for the lack of

courtesy she had been given. There wasn't a long line of women waiting to go home with a garbage man soon after meeting him. As such,
he decided it was in his best interest to ensure she didn't leave mad.

Trying to smooth it over, he commented soothingly, "Hey, it's not
like that. Why don't you write down your name and number and let
daddy make it up to you?"

She stepped back and shot him a "Negro please" look. Not to
worry. He was in his domain and continued as though ignorant of
everything that had transpired.

"Come on," he pleaded, "let daddy show you it ain't like you
think."

She didn't go easy and looked at him as if to say, "I dare you try
that crap on me." He had become adapt at rejection and ignored her
facial expression while continuing to lay on the charm. He could see
he was winning her over. The come on was definitely getting the better of her.

Trying to act as if she was still upset, she replied, "Oh yeah, then
how is it?"

He pulled her close and whispered while kissing her neck. "It's just
that right now daddy's in a bad way. I mean a bad way ain't the word.
Baby, if I don't get to work on time, I'm gonna be robbing banks by
this time tomorrow."

His comments made her laugh. He privately congratulated himself. Daddy had done it again. He thought he should change his name
to Mickey Ds because he had just satisfied another customer. He took
this opportunity to grab a scrap of paper and pen then hand it to her.

She quickly scribbled, *Rene Sims, 555-3701.*

He took the paper and slid it into his front pocket as both headed
out the door.

CHAPTER 2

As usual, Batman arrived at work at exactly seven a.m. for his six a.m. shift. Everyone was used to him coming late. The way he saw it, the truck didn't leave the yard until five minutes after seven, so to hell with showing up at six for debriefing and check out. The nerve of his boss thinking he had to debrief a grown man on how to empty a garbage can. *Some people will do anything to look important.* He had been on the county's garbage crew for close to three years. If someone had asked him four years ago about working on a garbage truck, he would have said, "Hell no, I won't go." Prior to it, he worked for two years washing cars at a local Ford dealership. To make a long story short, they fired him for insubordination. If someone were to ask him, his version would be it was because he refused to go along with Mr. Charlie's program.

Afterwards, he resolved not to take another job until he'd drawn down his unemployment. What he didn't know was they had changed the rules. That freakin' Clinton welfare reform crap. Steel Bill was his man and all, but he hadn't done a brotha no favors with that reform crap. It used to be that they wanted proof you were looking. Now, in order to keep from paying you, they sent you out to the worst jobs they could find. If you refuse the gig, and they hope you did, you are automatically discontinued. If it had been Mississippi, he would have been sent to the chicken factory. If it had been Cali, he would have been picking fruit. North Carolina…picking tobacco. Since it was Miami, they sent him to the garbage department. With no options, he complied.

Most folks look down on garbage workers. They wonder why anyone with any skills whatsoever would do it. However, once there he convinced himself it wasn't that bad of a gig. If you're able to get past the pride thing, the rest is down hill. In fact, it fit his mantra to a tee. It didn't require a lot of responsibility beyond making sure all the garbage was out of the can prior to throwing it back and that it was left upside down on rainy days. He got to ride half the time and walk the other, so it kept him in good shape. It was outdoor work, and it allowed him to see the city. Although it was as far as you could get from being the President, it got him to the driveway of the President's mansion. The hours were six until three, which afforded him the opportunity to have his evenings free. He was off on week-ends and holidays. There was potential for upward mobility if anyone considered driving rather than riding on the back of the truck upward. And the pay wasn't all that bad when compared to flipping burgers.

He walked through the export gate and saw his truck approach-ing. He worked on a four-man crew. Emerson, his direct supervisor, always drove while he, Abdullah and Pedro rotated on the back. Emerson had worked on the crew for thirty-one years and was approaching retirement. He was the grandfather of the yard and though unpopular, was grudgingly respected by everyone. That was, everyone except Batman. Slightly built and of dark olive complexion, Emerson constantly bragged about being of Indian descent. To him the need to identify with something other than being black was as dear as life itself. It was evident by his black stringy hair and dwarfish looks that he indeed was mixed with something. The thing was, Batman was there to dump garbage and could care less. He was sold on the notion that of all the places in the world where race mattered, working on the back of a freaking garbage truck wasn't one of them.

Pedro, the youngest in age, had joined the crew around the time Batman had. Pedro stood two inches taller than Emerson with hair just as black, only more tightly curled. This was his first job in the United States, and he acted as if it would be his last. Considering how happy he was to be in the States and working on a garbage truck, Batman could only surmise how bad things were in his coun-try.

Abdullah, on the other hand, couldn't wait to quit. The constant look of anger always strewn across his bald plate made one wonder why he even bothered to show up. Having converted to Islam while up the road, he had been on the crew for eighteen months. He would have been out of there, but was compelled to stay until his probation was up.

This morning Pedro took the first shift riding. The four were responsible for the Coral Gables route, which they divided into three shifts. Except for Emerson, one person rode first and then rotated with another until they finished.

Waving, Batman hailed for Emerson to slow down while he jumped on. Emerson's normal practice was to pull down to first gear while Batman would run and jump on. Instead, Emerson pulled to a complete stop and leaned out the window.

Batman saw something was on his mind as he greeted, "What's up, Cochise," then looked to the back and added, "what's up, guys?"

Cochise was the nickname he had given Emerson because of his always bringing up that Indian foolishness. He knew it got under his skin and was glad it did. To be honest, when it came to pissing off wanna-bees, Batman aimed to please.

"I've told you before, my name isn't Cochise," Emerson said, the pulse quickening in his temple. "Call me my name or don't call me nothing at all. And if your illiterate ass can't remember, then write it down."

"O.K., what's up nothing?"

Emerson stared at him with pure hatred then spat out the window in Batman's general direction, careful not to get too close. "What's up is Mr. Gonzales has the hots for you. He said for me to send you to him as soon as you arrived."

Irritated by his condescending tone, Batman decided to give it back to him. He understood there was nothing that made a supervisor madder than when a subordinate was insubordinate and took pride in being as insubordinate as a subordinate could be.

"Oh, he did—did he?" he asked, feigning ignorance. "What does he want, to give me my bonus? Or is he worried about the EEO suit I filed about all the racism in this damn yard?"

Emerson was not one to get into long debates. He felt as though Batman was beneath him, and it was a task to talk to him at all. "I don't know what he wants, and I don't care. All I know is you're to see him."

"Is that right?" Batman responded, not quite ready to let it die. "How about I click my heels three times and repeat I wanna go home. I wanna go home. I wanna go home. And see if he pops up?"

Pedro and Abdullah watched intently as Emerson and Batman went at it. Pedro, being an immigrant from some poor country in Central America, disliked any confrontation. He seemingly thought or had been advised fighting would hurt his chances of obtaining full citizenship. As a result, he was the butt of most of the jokes and the recipient of all the shit details Gonzales couldn't pawn off on anyone else.

Abdullah, on the other hand, watched to see who was real and who was faking. Slim but ripped with muscles from endless sessions of lifting weights in the prison yard, Abdullah tugged his shirttail to his face and wiped away the beads of perspiration that had begun to form. He had no great love for either of man; for all he cared, they could both go to hell.

Batman looked up at Emerson on the verge of becoming miffed. For a second, he thought about pulling out one of his niggas. Just like Master Card, he never left home without them. One was dumb nigga, which he carried him in his left pocket. The other was smart nigga which he carried his right pocket. Whenever he wanted to sandpaper somebody's ass, he'd pull one of them out. The dumb nigga played the nut role. The smart nigga just played the nut.

"Look, I came to work to work, and not to be harassed," he said, ready to go into his right pocket. "If that O-Yay wants to see me, then he knows where I'm at."

Finished, he took his place on the truck. He could see Emerson staring him down through his mirror, not quite sure what to do.

Emerson knew Gonzales was sure to chew him out when he returned, but he also knew that for better or for worse, Batman said what he meant and meant what he said. Deciding it better to let Gonzales handle his own affairs, he pulled off.

By 1:30 they had finished their route and were headed back to the yard area. As was their custom, they stopped by the burger pit on 25th and 14th Ave. After receiving their orders, they took a seat at a four-person table near the front by the plate glass window. Parked outside was a City of Miami police cruiser with a brother seated behind the steering wheel, appearing to be eating his lunch and listening to the radio. For a brief moment, he and Batman made eye contact and nodded their acknowledgement.

The tension from the morning disagreement hung heavy in the air. It was obvious Emerson and Batman were doing all they could not to speak to each other. Abdullah, believing fast food to be the means by which Mr. Charlie poisoned black minds, read silently in a corner. Pedro, attempting to achieve some semblance of normality, made small talk. However, it was obvious he was upset.

Changing the conversation, Pedro asked Batman in his heavy Central American accent, "Mr. Gonzales not gone fire you, no?"

By now the day had taken its toll on Batman. Between Nedra's smart, funny ways and Emerson's wanna be foolishness, what was a brotha to do but pull out of the right pocket. Thought touched, it bothered Batman that Pedro was concerned about his welfare. With all he had to deal with, trying to make it in a foreign land while taking crap on the yard, he shouldn't have had to worry about whether he would have a job the next day.

Responding to Pedro but clearly speaking to Emerson, he replied, "Pedro, I could give less than a damn about that O-Yay." Careful not to use the N-word because it upset Abdullah, he continued, "He may scare these other Negroes, but I could care less than a damn about him."

As soon as it left Batman's mouth, Emerson was out of his seat. Furious, his expression startled the people seated nearest to them.

Out of the corner of his eye, Batman saw customers moving to give them room.

Pointing his finger in the direction of Batman's face, Emerson screamed, "That's it. That's the last time you're getting away with calling me a name. I'm telling you for the last time, I ain't nobody's nigga. If you don't know it by now, I'm three fourths Seminole."

Emerson's use of the word "nigga" had caught Abdullah's attention. On any other occasion, Abdullah would have taken offense. Batman was sure Abdullah would take it up with Emerson later. However, right here and right now this wasn't Abdullah's issue. It was between Batman and Emerson.

Still seated, Batman couldn't believe this old man had tried to front on him. Any thought of playing a zone was quickly dismissed. This occasion was one in which the only thing that would do was a man-to-man full court press. He'd been taught to respect his elders, but he wasn't about to let some Uncle Tom garbage truck driver embarrass him. He rose from his seat to where he was within arm's length of Emerson.

Speaking slowly, calmly, and as contemptuously as he could manage, Batman grudgingly conceded, "O.K., you're Seminole." He waited as Emerson breathed a sigh of victory then added, "But in my book that just makes you a prairie NIGGAH."

Everyone's eyes locked on the two of them. Abdullah had closed his book and sat silently in his seat. Pedro looked frantic. Not knowing exactly what to do, Pedro slid from his seat and stepped in between Emerson and Batman. All the while, unbeknownst to either of the two combatants, the brother police officer, who had been seated outside, had seen the disturbance and walked up behind Batman. He stepped from behind Batman to where Pedro stood between the two of them. Batman saw the policeman's expression and immediately knew who he was gunning for.

The police officer spoke to no one in particular but looked directly at Batman and asked, "Is there a problem?" He placed a hand to his night stick and added, "Cause if there is, I'm the one who's going to fix it."

Batman was unfazed. No one said anything, and Emerson and Batman continued to lock eyes. Pedro, shaking like a leaf on a tree and afraid either of their arrest would negatively affect his immigration status, was the first to respond. His nervousness served to make his broken English worse.

"No mistah offisah, everyting is very very alright. Please, please everything is very alright," he repeated unconvincingly. He turned from the officer to the other patrons and said, "Please forgeeve us, please please forgeeve us. We not mean to disturb nobody."

The officer held his gaze on Batman, weighing whether he was worth the hassle. Abdullah was a veteran of the law enforcement system, knew how police officers thought. He figured the prey was the young black male. He rose from his seat, moved stealth-like to where Pedro had previously been standing then stopped and looked directly into the eyes of the officer.

In his low baritone voice, he stated, "We need to be getting back to the yard." He walked past the officer toward the exit. Batman knew the script and fell in line behind him as they all dispersed.

Within five minutes of loading on, they were back in the yard. Batman had hoped to get in and out to avoid seeing Gonzales. He had endured enough drama for the day and didn't need any more. However, no sooner had they packed the truck away for the weekend did Gonzales show up.

Gonzales and he had been at odds since day one. Not only did Gonzales's attitude rankle Batman, but also his looks did. Gonzales suffered from chronic acne, which as Batman had previously advised him served to make his face look like an unmade bed. He had come over during the boatlift when Fidel Castro had emptied his asylums and prisons and freed them to become America's problem. Through the aid of his Cuban brethren, he had managed to secure a job and work his way up in the garbage department. He considered himself a hard-ass and ran the yard as if a dictator.

The problem Batman had with him was the same as he had with

most other Cubans in South Florida. They supposedly braved high seas and other dangers to escape a dictatorship; however, they would get here and try to establish one in Miami. In his opinion, they generally looked down their noses at blacks and other Hispanics as if Cubans were superior. *Go figure. Why leave a communist country risking death to get to a democracy just to set up a banana republic?*

Speaking in broken English made worse by his heavy Cuban accent, Gonzales walked right up to where Batman was standing. "Hey, Osborne," he addressed him with disdain, "deed not Emmason tell you I say for you to see me?"

As he had in the past, Batman saw an opportunity to make his speech an issue. "No hablo Espanol," he replied, still hot from his run in with Emerson. "Haven't you heard? This is an English speaking only work site. That's right, you can't empty garbage if you can't speak English."

Gonzales wasted little time entering the fray. This was right up his alley. "Listen, Osborne, I no have no crap from you. I run your ass outta dis yard. You always late and you always cause trouble. You late for your sheeft this morning, no? I know, I fire you. You fired. Geet out of here and not come back. Go, go now before I kick you out myself." As he spoke, he waved his hands and gestured wildly.

Offended Gonzales was in his space, Batman decided to ratchet it up a notch. He changed his tone so as to make it clear to Gonzales he was about to get bum rushed. "Gonzales, unless you want your kids to be orphans and your wife to be a widow, you best get out of my face. And as far as being fired, I'm not even worried." Hesitating while he backed off, he continued, "I'm going to give you a new word to add to your American vocabulary. If my math is right, that means you now have two. And you don't even have to thank me for it. It's called Union. That's U-YON, union. Look it up in the dictionary, and it will tell you I'm not going a damn place until I'm good and ready. And you know why? Because it's rough on rats and tough on cats, that's why."

Not deterred in the least, Gonzales reached in his shirt pocket and thrust Batman a letter. "Dis is for you. You fired. Go to the county on Monday and dey gone tell you the same thing. I da damn boss of dis yard. I told them to take you or else we fire you."

Batman grudgingly took the note then turned and stalked off. *It wouldn't be so bad if Gonzales did fire me. I'm getting tired of all the crap anyway.* Dismissing the thought, he turned the envelope over in his hand to see if it offered a clue as to its contents. Not recognizing anything but his name on the front, he opened it. It was brief and to the point but explained why Gonzales had been on the rag all day. The letter stated that his EEO complaint from six months earlier had been forwarded to a counselor. He recognized the name and remembered having spoken to her briefly. It directed that he was to show up at the county personnel office at eight a.m. to discuss his grievance. He was to see the same counselor, Ms. Andrea Rivera.

CHAPTER 3

Nedra peeped around the corner to see how many patients were waiting in the lobby. To her dismay, the clinic was still full. Two-thirty in the afternoon, if she didn't get them out soon, she'd be late for her four o'clock hair appointment. Accounting for the weekend traffic, she reasoned she needed to be enroute by three-thirty. She had made the appointment two weeks earlier in preparation of the date she had tonight. Brain, a police officer she met at the clinic, would be picking her up at nine for a night on the town. She'd met him in the clinic when he'd brought some inmates over to be tested. Needing them seen quickly so that he could take them to the courthouse for arraignment, she had assisted. It had been six weeks since they had first started seeing each other regularly. In her mind, the relationship was growing stronger with each passing day.

The excitement of having a new man in her life caused her to reflect on her last steady relationship. It had been three years since she had been in one. It had ended in disaster when she found out her then fiancée had been unfaithful. Unable to reconcile his behavior, she had called off the wedding. Subsequently, she took a new job with the federal government and was assigned to the Miami Sexually Transmitted Disease Program.

Brian was everything she had hoped and prayed for. After all this time, God was actually granting her prayer. Intelligent and athletic, he loved to read. Once, they had spent an entire evening parked on Biscayne Bay in his cruiser with him reading to her. Along with that, he was extremely good looking. He sported a small scar above his right cheek, which she thought extremely manly. She found him attractive beyond any man she had ever met. Tall and handsome, he sported a bald fade. But best of all, he was single. Single and free. She thought that hard to believe, considering that most black men were either in jail, headed for jail or married. And the ones not already married had other tastes for pleasure. But not Brian. He was a man of conviction and purpose. As he told her, it was his conviction to uphold the law that had led him into law enforcement. Over the time they had spent together, she had not only come to respect him but to admire him.

There was no doubt about it. She knew Brian was the one. The person God had put here to be her soul mate. He was on the hook and only needed to be reeled in. That's why it was important for her to look her best. That's why she needed to make her appointment. She scratched the two inches of new growth just to confirm she needed to get those old braids out and a relaxer in.

As the first-line supervisor, she supervised the sexually transmitted disease clinic. That meant she couldn't leave until the last patient was seen. Her duties required she assign and review cases of subordinate employees. Her employees, disease intervention specialists, were referred to as DIS within the health department. Each DIS was responsible for interviewing patients infected with syphilis, gonorrhea, or HIV. During the interview, the DIS was expected to solicit sexual partners of the infected person. After the interview, they went into the field and made home visits in order to locate the sex partners who had been named. Once located, the partners were directed to the clinic for examination and treatment. Anyone who came in because of being contacted by a DIS was considered a referral. Referrals had priority over patients who walked in. For easy identification, referrals were registered with pink medical records, while walk-ins were registered with blue records.

Nedra approached the admissions window and saw a stack of pink records. Her first thought was that her employees were messing off again. They knew referrals required at a minimum examination and treatment by the physician, which meant they were to be taken care of first. She normally refrained from patient contact, but knew if she didn't intervene fast, she would not get out in time. Reaching through the check-in window, she grabbed the handful of pink records. After a quick examination, she concluded most had returned for test results only. Because the results were negative, it was not necessary for them to be provided by her staff. She quickly scanned the hall, saw the clinic nurse approaching and pulled her aside. After explaining the situation, she directed her to provide the patients with their results. Walking briskly, she entered the employee lounge and summoned a male DIS from another team.

"Go over to the Hadley Building and get three people to come cover the clinic," she directed. "I'm going to do this syphilis interview. By the time I finish, I want this clinic to be empty."

He didn't want to be the bearer of bad news. "Who should I get? Everyone's on field today."

Nedra knew she had placed him in a bad situation but didn't have time to go back and forth. Clearly rushed, she replied, "I don't care who you get. Get the first three people you see whether they're on field or not. Tell them what I said and for them to get over here. If they give you any lip, come get me." Finished, she returned to the patient waiting area and called out above the noise, "Number 92...number 92."

A young African-American female with braided extensions stood and walked toward her. She was dressed in a hot red halter-top and tight fitting blue jeans. Around her wrist dangled an army of cheap silver and gold bracelets. The jeans showed off her long legs and slim waist, which caused the males to stare as she passed. Aware of the attention, she smiled and attempted to walk sexier.

"Hey, why don't you give me them digits after the doctor clean you up?" replied one male patient. The clinic burst out in laughter as she continued into the hallway.

She reached Nedra and said softly, "I'm number 92."

Nedra held out her hand and replied, "Hi, I'm Nedra, and I'm a counselor here. Follow me."

Seated in an interviewing room, Nedra looked over the young lady's chart, again. After committing the young lady's name to memory, she began, "Jackie, why did you come in today?"

Jackie wasted little time in answering. She had been in the clinic the better part of four hours and was anxious to leave. It was Friday, and she had places to go and people to see.

"A man came by my house and said I needed to come in. He said somebody I had sex with was infected. I told him it couldn't be me because the only person I've had sex with is my baby's daddy. I called him, and he said he don't got nothing."

Rushed for time, Nedra decided to cut to the chase. She knew a complete and thorough syphilis interview could take up to hours. The abbreviated version only required she provide the patient with the important information to prevent re-infection and get the names of her sex partners.

"O.K. Jackie, listen to me. Everything we talk about is confidential. That means no one will know except people working to help cure you of this infection or the people you go out and tell. Do you understand?"

Allowing time for her to nod she understood, Nedra continued. "The doctors took your blood and tested it for syphilis. The test came back positive, so they're going to give you some medicine. First, I have to talk to you. We have to talk about who you've been having sex with."

Jackie had been to the clinic several times before and knew that acknowledging sex partners could mean an even longer stay. She had decided in advance to be deceptive. "I told you I haven't had sex with anybody but my baby's daddy."

Nedra didn't want to lose the opportunity to elicit sex partners by challenging the patient. Instead, she decided to move on and come back to it later. "O.K., we'll talk about that later. Let me ask you, what do you know about syphilis?"

"I know it's a sex disease, that's about it," Jackie answered, knowing she would probably be there a long time.

"O.K., that good—that's real good." Nedra paused long enough to take a breath. "Syphilis is a sexually transmitted disease. When I say that, I mean that the only way you can get it is by having sex with someone who's infected. That means someone gave you this while you all were having sex. The good part is, we know you have it and can give you some medicine for it. The bad part is, if we don't get everyone you've come in contact with, you can get re-infected."

Nedra stopped momentarily, reached into her desk and pulled out a sheaf of cards. Each card had a picture of signs and symptoms of a person infected with syphilis. One by one, she proceeded to show Jackie the pictures while asking if she had ever noticed the symptoms on her or anyone she'd had sex with.

Jackie saw one in particular and commented, "I had a sore like that. I thought it was just a hair bump. After a while it went away."

"Well the sore does go away, but that doesn't mean you're cured," Nedra replied, making note in the chart. "Syphilis is a blood disease. After the sore leaves, it's still in your blood."

Satisfied she had collected all the symptom information, Nedra returned to her previous line of questioning. She placed the pictures into the drawer and took out a plain sheet of paper to write on.

"O.K. Jackie, we need to talk about your sex partners. How many people have you had sex with in the last year?"

"Ms. Health Department Lady, I told you one," Jackie answered defiantly. "That's my baby daddy. And I don't mess with him no more, so I can't get infected."

"O.K. what's his name."

"Darrell."

"Darrell what?"

Jackie knew very well she was lying. She and Darrel hadn't had sex in over a year. Furthermore, unknown to him, he wasn't her baby's daddy. She had chosen him based on his employment status and nothing more. He had been quite generous, and she didn't want to ruin it by having the health department tell him she had given his name. On the other hand, the lady said everything was confidential. Maybe she could play along and hurry up and get out.

Jackie paused then answered, "Darrell Morgan. Why you need all that? You not going to tell him I was here are you?"

"I told you everything we talk about is confidential. That means your name won't be given to anyone. If we have to contact him, we will do just like we did you. We'll tell him he's come in contact with someone who's infected but won't give him the name. Now tell me, when was the last time you had sex with him?"

Jackie took time to think before she responded.

"About two months ago."

Nedra exhaled slowly and laid her pen down. She stared at Jackie. This was a trick she often used to extract the truth from patients. As an experienced interviewer, she knew when someone was lying. Moreover, she assumed more often than not that most patients lied about their sex lives. Discussing sex in general is sensitive, discussing who you're having sex with, what type sex you're having, and how often you're having it is even more sensitive. However, the bottom line was, Nedra was responsible for getting contacts named and treated. Her ability to do so was reflected in her evaluation and ultimately in her promotions. Nedra had qualms about lying or misleading patients, but she felt compelled to do so, believing it was the only way she could get to the truth. Having no direct proof, she would use her knowledge of how the infection is transmitted to try and trip Jackie up.

Lying she continued, "Jackie, we have a problem. I'm looking at the info you gave me on Darrell there's no way he gave you this. You got this from somebody else. Now tell me honestly, who else have you had sex with?"

"Nobody. I'm telling you he's the only one."

Deciding you could catch more flies with honey than vinegar, Nedra took a different approach. "Jackie, I'm telling you he's not the one. Now I'm a sister from the old school. I saw the way those guys were looking at you. Girl, every one of those guys wanted to get with you. Now I'm not nearly as fine as you, and I know how guys worry me about having sex. I can't imagine them not bothering you all the time. C'mon now, tell me what I already know. Don't worry, they'll never know you gave their names."

Flattered by Nedra's compliments, Jackie admitted, "Well there is a couple of other guys; but I haven't been with them all that much. Two of them are married. I don't want to get them in trouble."

"That's o.k., they won't know you gave their names. And if you don't tell, and they will give it to their wives, they're going to be in more trouble."

Nedra obtained the names and locating information then walked Jackie to the treatment nurse. Prior to leaving, Nedra handed Jackie a handful of condoms and instructed her to use them. She gathered her notes to turn them over to an employee to follow up on. She opened the door and saw one of her employees waiting out in the hall. With little thought, she said, "Janet, come here. I have a case for you to work."

Janet had been waiting in the hall hoping to leave. She was severely overworked and had no intention of taking on a new case until she had caught up. However, she knew it would do no good to try to reason with Nedra. Everyone at the health department privately despised her for her zeal in trying to get ahead.

Nedra took the information she had gathered and handed it to Janet. "Make sure you follow up on this pronto," she instructed. "Her HIV test results aren't back, but when they come back be sure to post them."

Janet took the case and silently nodded as Nedra gave instructions then turned and headed back to her office. Nedra grabbed her purse and ran to the patient area. Seeing it was empty, she continued through and out the door.

CHAPTER 4

Batman made it home around eight-thirty that night. The trip home had taken close to five hours. He and Nedra lived in El Portal, which was two blocks off the bus line. On a normal day, he could have made it entirely by bus in one and a half hours. However, it wasn't a normal day. This was Friday and that meant it was his day to get blasted. He lived for the weekends, and although he often started on Thursday, Friday was his official start. He had walked from the yard down 14th Ave. to the Jackson Memorial Metro Rail station. Affectionately known by Miami residents as Metro Fail, he took the Northbound up to 64th Street. From there he caught the bus over to Scott Project.

He stopped by the dope man's house for what he thought was thirty minutes, only to realize later that he had actually stayed three hours. Dopeman and he had been doing business for over two years and had developed their own bond. After filling his order, Dopeman had offered him a hit on the house. Of course it was a portion of what he had shorted him on his bags over the years. Batman accept-ed, and they spent the next couple of hours smoking gungi and lis-tening to old Earth, Wind and Fire albums. In between, they settled most of the free world's problems. The bulk of their conversing was spent debating the pros and cons of smoking reefer versus crack from a businessperson's perspective.

Combined, their knowledge could have been used to write a dis-sertation—in one room you had the extensive, comprehensive and combined knowledge of both the supplier and the consumer. Dopeman sold both and was adamant that crack was the better busi-ness product. The high addiction rate negated having to attract new clients. As a result, the market demand was constant. It was cheap and relatively easy to produce and distribute. Batman's position was reefer was better and that Dopeman was ignoring the marginal costs associated with crack. In the old days, everybody smoked reefer. Even the President, his boy Steel Bill, admitted trying it. Everybody liked it, but nobody sold their body or robbed their mama. The best part from a businessperson's perspective was no one did drive-by shootings because of it.

Not deterred, Dopeman's position was the price elasticity of demand, or the percent change in volume resulting from a percentage change in price, favored crack over reefer. It was due to the addict's inability or unwillingness to substitute in consumption. The reefer user could very well substitute alcohol or some other drug—not so with crack. The immediate intense high couldn't be compared with anything outside of Mexican heroin. Batman conceded this point, but not his position, asserting the marginal costs that Dopeman still seemed to ignore.

Unable to convince the other, they decided to call a truce. Batman had thanked him for his graciousness and decided it was time to make the last leg home. Prior to leaving, he borrowed some cologne and sprayed some on. He didn't want to hear Nedra's mouth when he got in. He felt there was no worse way for a grown man to blow a good high than by having someone scold you like a child. Nedra knew he smoked and was disapproving of it. She was always ridiculing that he was a dope head without a cause. For the sake of peace in the neighborhood, he ignored her. More than once he'd explained that it wasn't that he needed it, but just that he enjoyed it. For his part, he chose instead to believe that there were three levels of drug use: recreational, habitual, and clinical. Recreational being you enjoyed it, habitual being you desired it, and clinical being you needed it. Him? He was somewhere between recreational and habitual.

Upon entering the house, he headed straight for his bedroom. His agenda called for listening to Frankie Beverly and Maze until falling out for a nap. After his nap, he had planned to take a shower and head for the clubs. He walked through his bedroom on to the bathroom to pay the water bill. He finished then returned to the bedroom. Initially, his high had made him blind to the difference in how his room currently looked as opposed to how he had left it that morning. Slowly reality set in. Speaking to himself, he commented, "What the hell happened here?" Gone were the piles of dirty clothes. Gone were the dirty dishes left lying all over the place. The bed had been made with fresh sheets and the clutter had been replaced with order. Worse yet, the room smelled of air freshener and ammonia.

He proceeded straight to Nedra's room, knocked and walked in before receiving an answer and asked, "Hey, you know what happened to my bedroom?"

She smiled like the keeper of the key to a hidden treasure. "Sure I know what happened. What happened is I cleaned it up. Don't thank me."

Thanking her was the furthest thing from his mind. Although he appreciated the gesture, they had a rule never to enter into the other's space without permission. The reefer had his thoughts going in every direction. He returned to the conversation at hand. "Sure. But why?"

Smugly, Nedra answered, "Why is because I have a special guest coming over, and I didn't want him seeing it that way."

The reefer had him running about five seconds behind in the conversation. With some effort, he managed to catch-up. "O.K., but tell me why would he want to see my bedroom?"

"Because he's a law enforcement officer, and because of your bedroom, the whole house reeks of reefer."

The reefer kicked into high gear and caused his mind to move even slower. The five second delay seemed to have grown to fifty-five. He felt like he was running in quick sand. He tried to decipher her last statement about someone being a law enforcement officer when it hit him. "Oh he's nine?"

"No he's not nine," she said in opposition to his characterization. "He's a law enforcement officer, and he's due here any moment. If you don't want to go to jail, then I suggest you go and take a good shower. You smell horrible, like a mixture of garbage, reefer and cheap cologne."

Batman smiled and stuck his chest out like Superman. "I was planning on showering after my nap, but for you I'll do it now. Never let it be said that I stood in the way of you reeling in the big fish."

True to his word, he returned to his room and took a long shower. By the time he finished, he was only marginally high. He was tempted to burn a joint, but had no desire to jeopardize Nedra's date with her new boyfriend. Instead, he settled for Frankie Beverly and a nap.

No sooner had his head touched the pillow, he was out like a lamp. Two hours, but what seemed like two minutes later, he was awakened by the banging at his door like a wild banshee. Immediately, he knew it was Nedra. He had become as familiar with the banging as he was with her voice. By the way she was banging, he could tell she was excited.

"Batman!!! Batman!!!! You woke?"

He rolled over. "Sure Nedra, I'm woke. Come on in."

She opened the door and peeped in to make sure he was presentable. He thought to himself that it would have been hard to explain to a new boyfriend had he been naked. Satisfied he was fit for viewing, she slowly stepped into the room. Behind her followed a tall black male in a police officer's uniform.

"Batman, I want you to meet Brian." Quite proud of him she joked, "I told him all about you, and he's agreed not to hold it against you."

They both laughed at her feeble attempt at humor. Batman was still trying to bring his eyes into focus. He sat upright on the bed, leaned over and instinctively extended his hand to him.

"Nice to meet you, Officer Brian," he said like a child on a field trip to the Police Department.

"Nice to meet you," the officer replied, echoing Batman's greeting.

As they shook hands, the officer's face came into focus. Batman was sure he had seen him before. About the same time that Batman's memory placed him, the officer's did likewise. Nedra, ever the investigator, saw the looks and knew exactly what they meant.

She placed her hands over her mouth. "Don't tell me you know each other. Oh no. Batman, for Pete's sake, tell me you haven't been to jail."

Batman intentionally delayed his response, giving her time to consider the possibility that he had been arrested and not told her. Satisfied he'd delivered the intended response, he replied, "Who me? You know better than that. It's rough on rats and tough on cats, but I'm not about to go out like no punk."

Brian interrupted, saying, "We met at lunch. He was about to take out some poor old brother when I intervened."

Forgetting his name, Batman replied, "Mr. Policeman, if only you knew. He's black, but he's definitely no brother. If you knew that guy for one day, you'd pay me to kick his butt. Anyway, what I was planning on doing to him was worse than a butt kicking."

Brian smiled. "Even so, you can't go around fighting—especially in public."

Batman didn't attempt to defend his behavior any further. "I hear you." He decided it was better to change the subject. "So where is the happy couple heading tonight to get their groove on?"

Sounding dejected, Nedra replied, "That's just it. Brian has been taken advantage of again by his friends. One of his patrol buddies called in sick and Brian agreed to cover for him. He's always covering for them. So now he only has a couple of hours before he has to be back on duty. We decided we'd spend our time watching T.V. What about you?"

"Well, I was planning on anointing myself with oil, reading my Bible and praying until I fell asleep. But I guess now I'll ride out to Big Daddy's so you can watch T.V. in private." Batman laughed. "Don't thank me."

Nedra and Brian looked at each other and laughed. Everyone had gotten the point. Mildly embarrassed, Nedra commented, "Quit lying, you go to Big Daddy's every Friday. Where else could you find those scum bags you keep bringing up in here?"

Brain or no Brian, Batman wasn't about to let her have the last word. "As we say in the yard, one man's trash is another man's treasure."

The two turned to leave when Brian commented, "Nedra says you like to shoot hoops. Where do you play?"

"Allen Park on Northeast 19th and 167. Stop by tomorrow morning around nine if you have a mind to. We run some pretty good games, and the competition is o.k."

"I've been under the weather the past two weeks. However, as soon as I feel better, don't be surprised if you look up and see me," he said then walked out.

CHAPTER 5

Batman rolled into Big Daddy's just when the party was hitting high gear. It took him fifteen minutes to park and another five minutes to travel the four blocks from where he had found a space. Outside the club, people were huddled in small groups chatting and laughing. Inside the club, people were packed shoulder to shoulder like sardines. There was barely room to move about. The DJ was mixing a track by Wu Tang Klan and everyone was hopping. The small dance floor, flooded over with dancers, sent people dancing between tables.

He felt a hand on his shoulder and turned to see it was his homeboy, Shag. Shag stood dancing with a female who Batman recognized to be a regular. The smile on Shag's face signaled he was close to scoring. Batman threw up his hand and shouted over the crowd noise, "What's up?"

Shag smiled even wider and mouthed his famous line, "Pimpin' 'em hard my brother."

Batman elbowed his way through the crowd until he was able to secure a place at the bar. It was a perfect place from which to survey the crowd. He knew the bartender from his frequent visits. They made eye contact, and Batman held up one finger for the bartender to bring his usual, Grand Mariner with water on the side. While waiting for his drink, he began to formulate his list of potential pick-ups.

His first inclination was always to look for women traveling in groups. Ladies in groups of three or four were ideal. Past experience had taught him that they were the easiest to pickup. Less than three and they felt pressured not to leave their girlfriend alone. The saying "we came together and we're leaving together," prevailed. More than four and peer pressure kicked in. No one could be sure someone wouldn't talk later about them playing the whore role. In Batman's estimation, women, even friends, were in constant competition with one another. They would never admit it, but it was never the less true. Men knew this and understood it made them vulnerable. By playing to it, he and other males were able to capitalize on this vulnerability. He had more than once explained the nuances to Shag.

"You see, all groups have a pecking order. It's subjective in nature but objectively maintained. That's to say there's no rhyme or reason to how it comes about, but once it is established, the persons at the top of the pecking order seeks to ensure they stay at the top. The key for the guy is to identify the female in the group least likely to get noticed then shower her with attention. Her friends, ahead of her in the order, thinking they are more deserving, are internally challenged to maintain the status quo. The result is, they are willing to do what's necessary to redirect the male attention based on the established order. Hence, the vulnerability."

It didn't take long for him to find what he was looking for. In fact, he saw two tables that he considered equally promising. On these occasions, he would take his first shot at the one with the female he found most attractive. That way, if things didn't work out, he could drop down to choice number two.

Drink finished, he headed to the table right off the dance floor. He had noticed a young woman sitting with two friends and had watched as they alternatively danced with different guys. She, however, had yet to dance. Nursing her drink, she sat alone in her chair, moving with the rhythm of the beat. Her grooving with the music signaled she liked to dance but had either not been asked or not accepted. This was Big Daddy's, a club where even the most raunchy got asked.

Batman intentionally arrived at her table at the same time her friends were returning from the dance floor. In this case, he considered this definitely to his advantage. As mentioned, her dancing in her seat meant she had not been asked or had not accepted. He'd seen enough guys approach the table to know it was the latter. Therefore, he knew his best chance was not to ask her but to use the influence of her friends.

He kneeled between her two friends as they took their seats and asked, "Hey, what's your friend's name?"

The first to speak, and obviously the leader of the group, replied, "Why don't you ask her? She has a mouth. What, she doesn't look like she knows her name?"

Batman smiled. "No, that's not it. It's just that she looks frightened, and I don't want to scare her."

The three of them looked at each other as if to say "how lame."

However, he wasn't deterred. He knew most guys considered coming on to women to be a dash, but for him it was a long distance run. The winning strategy was not to get out of the blocks fast, but to start slow, settle into a pace, and kick into full gear on the last leg.

"Are you all friends?" he asked conversationally. "Cause if you are, you're not doing a good job of being her friend."

It was her second friend's time now to chime in. Sounding upset, she said, "Now why would you say that? We haven't done anything to her."

"Sure you have. You've been treating her like the ugly step-sistah. You've been partying, and she hasn't danced once. If you were her friends, you would insist she danced at least once. Watch this…" He looked over to where she sat and asked, "Wanna dance?"

She smiled shyly and shook her head.

He turned back to her friends. "See what I mean? I wouldn't come to a club that's jumping like this and not make my friend dance. And if he refused, I'd make him walk home."

The two females smiled at each other, knowing exactly what he was up to. However, they'd come out to have fun and saw no problem playing along. The one he assumed to be the leader looked over and chided, "Go ahead, Lisa. It's just a dance. You've been talking all week about coming here, and you haven't even gotten up. We'll watch your purse for you."

He didn't wait for her to put up any resistance but walked around the table and held out his hand. Although hesitant, she took it and rose from her seat. They stepped between tables as he led her to the dance floor. Up close, she looked even better than he had thought. Five feet eight inches tall with a medium frame, she was definitely well proportioned. Her dark-complexioned, oval face was enhanced by her glassy brown eyes and short jazzy haircut. She had what seemed to him to be a Halle Berry look. His eyes must have given him away, because she replied, "Did I pass?"

"Pass what?" he responded innocently.

"Your inspection," she replied, moving with the beat. "You were inspecting me weren't you?"

He decided honesty to be the best policy. "Assessing is more like it. I don't want you to think I'm a stalker or something, but I'm a sucker for looks."

They both laughed and continued through two tracks. Afterwards, she silently mouthed "thank you" and moved through the crowd back toward her table. He walked behind her, hoping not to lose her in the crowd. Once there, he saw only one of her friends waiting. He took this as an opportunity to sit and continue the conversation. He leaned over closely so she could hear him over the crowd noise. "You come here often?"

"Not really—you?"

Her reply gave him an opening to convey interest. "I used to, but whether I continue or not depends on you. In fact, I'm thinking about going to the manager and complaining about you."

She smiled. "And why would you do that?"

"Oh, I'm sure he'd like to know that you're about to make one of his best customers stop coming. I've been a regular here for years, looking for someone just like you. After seeing you, I must agree that good things come to those who wait."

Seemingly flattered, she said, "Wait a minute. I don't even know your name. And while you're funny and nice, I think I'd better pass on that line. I wouldn't want the manager mad at me."

"O.K., let's start over." Straight faced, he introduced himself using the tone and inflection of the cartoon character. "Hi I'm Batman."

She busted out laughing. "You're what?"

"Batman. You know. Like in Batman and Robin. That's what my friends call me. And you I would assume are Lisa?" She shook her head yes. "Great, that means my bat computer is providing good information. I wonder what other information it can get me on you."

Before he could continue, friend number two arrived back. He was hoping she would pull up a seat to allow him more time to close on the deal. However, without sitting, she signaled that they should be leaving. She must have been the driver, because everyone except him moved to gather their things.

Without thinking, he shot out, "Wait, I'm not ready. Here I am in the most important conversation of my life, and you all are leaving? Come on, I know you all are better than that?"

"Sorry, Batman, but I have to go," Lisa replied.

"O.K., but at least give me your telephone number before you leave. That way I can tell the police where to find the lady that stole my heart."

The two friends stood back to allow them room to talk. Lisa shook her head. "Sorry, Batman, but I'm married."

He attempted to make a sad face over the news. Then as sincerely as he could, he replied, "That's o.k., I'm not jealous."

Friend number two laughed. "No, but he is."

All three walked away, laughing at his come on. No doubt, he would be the object of their conversation during the ride home. Left to gather his thoughts, he headed for table two.

CHAPTER 6

Per usual, Batman knocked but didn't wait for a reply. He walked into Nedra's bedroom, dressed for his usual Saturday morning hoops game. Carrying a bowl of cereal, he moved to sit on her dresser. She lifted her head and smiled.

"Oh it's you," she said, fighting off the sleep. "What do you want?"

He smiled sheepishly. "I was headed out to shot hoops and decided to make sure you hadn't floated off during the night. Seems like ole boy has you walking on water."

"Get out of Dodge," she replied, coming full awake. "What do you know about anything?"

"I know a lot more than you give me credit for. Especially when it comes to that love thing. It looks to me like you're caught dead in the middle of that love thing." He changed his tone to one more serious. "I'm really happy for you. But all the same, I have to warn you to be careful not to hang your hat where you can't reach it."

Nedra and Batman were more than roommates, they had become true friends. He knew she had and would do anything for him, and he privately hoped she knew he would do the same for her. They were from the same hometown and had known each other since they were small children. She, two years his elder, was best friend to one of his closest female relatives. Nedra and his cousin had attended the same high school and both played on the basketball team. Upon graduation, she had gone off to the state university where she eventually graduated. During the period between her graduation from college and his from high school, he had come to Miami on a basketball scholarship from Dade Community College. His enrollment had lasted only one academic year. Not up to the challenge of schoolwork, he quit to pursue less stringent interests. Nedra, upon learning of her assignment to

Miami, contacted him. Subsequent to that, they agreed to become roommates.

Since that time he'd come to learn of her previous relationships. Most, if not all, had ended unhappily. The last had been particularly disastrous. Although she would differ, the combined effect of them had left her emotionally scarred. She had become cynical of black males in general, choosing to believe they were incapable of dealing with progressive, professional, African-American women, which, of course, she considered herself to be. Like many other sistahs, she believed her independence and spirit intimidated potential suitors. The thought that black males so needed power in their relationships led her to believe they would rather deal with a street sistah than a professional one.

With little to no success, Batman had spent hours trying to convince her that nothing could be further from the truth. The fact that a lot of sistahs are more highly educated and make more money than a lot of brothers was moot. He could honestly offer that of all the brothers he knew and had known, not one would have a problem cashing a sistah's check on Friday or driving her car around all week. Real brothers wanted their women to have material wealth and be intelligent. But real brother's weren't about to let anyone run them around because of it. In his opinion, too many sistah's attempted to define the relationship by what they had. Brothers could deal with that, but where the rubber hits the road, what you have isn't as important who you are.

He moved to the bed to sit beside her, took her hand and said, "Being in a relationship is no different than negotiating a contract. In a contract, each party negotiates for what they want and makes sure it's in before signing. Once the contract is signed, it's too late to negotiate for what you want. What I'm saying is just make sure what you want, is what he wants. Too many sistahs hang their hats on he'll come around to what I want. When he doesn't, they're left in the rain crying, 'Black men ain't shit.' When in reality, they'd hung their hats where they couldn't reach 'em."

Both looked at each other in silence. He knew he had brought her to a place where she didn't want to be—the intersection of Fantasy

Street and Reality Avenue. Where what you hope you got, and what you really got was manifested. Where the difference between fact and fiction was illuminated. As he spoke, he could see her pride rising up. He decided that pride didn't allow people to consider the pitfalls involved with going all out.

"Brian's not like that," she said resolutely. "I appreciate your concern, but I think I can take care of myself."

His speaking with her was not just for her sake, but his also. His conscience would have torn him apart if later things didn't work out between her and brain, and he hadn't attempted to school her.

"Nedra, this isn't about taking care of yourself. It's about being real and not ideal. That stuff sistahs read in magazines and watch on talk shows about love at first sight and living happily ever after is ideal, but not real. Being in a relationship where people lie, steal, kill and cheat is what's real. If you don't know by now, relationships are rough of rats and tough on cats."

Too sophisticated for a lecture to by anyone named after a comic book character, she replied combatively, "*Batman*, last time I checked I was wearing panties and not diapers. I walk around in three-inch heels and not in stride-rites baby shoes. This bra I'm wearing didn't come off the little miss isle. In case you haven't noticed, I'm a big girl. And this big girl knows what she wants and knows what she doesn't want. What I want is Brian. What I don't want is Batman playing the big brother role because I'm not hearing it."

"Nedra, call it what you want. That's just what I'm talking about. A sistah says they want a brother, but what they're saying is they want to get married and live a fantasy life. All I'm saying is a fantasy life is just that. It amazes me how sistahs watch this foolishness on Oprah and these other shows about how to get a husband. How in the world do you let someone without a husband tell you how to get one?"

"Wait one minute," she replied, cutting him off. "What the hell does Oprah Winfrey have to do with you walking into my room early on a Saturday morning and trying to lecture me as if you're somebody's daddy, or, better yet, an example of what a real brother should be? You talk about Oprah, but at least she attempts to educate herself on the issues before speaking, which is more than I can say for you or that cast of losers you deal with."

Over the course of the discussion, their voices had risen as they became entrenched in their positions. Batman could see they were headed for a knockdown drag out, which he neither wanted nor intended.

He softened his voice to lower the tension and made eye contact. "What I know is sistahs plan while brothers decide. A sistah meets a guy and plans how she's going to reel him in. After years of planning, he moves on and marries the next sistah he meets. The first sistah ends up angry, depressed and wondering what went wrong. The truth is, what was for her a plan was for him a decision. A brother can be with twenty sistahs over twenty years and just wake up one morning and decide out of the blue he's getting married. All I'm saying is if ole boy isn't ready then don't count your chickens."

Nedra scoffed at his remarks. "Brother man, thanks for the advice, but like the old folks say, 'Free advice is worth every penny you pay for it.'"

He realized that she hadn't accepted anything he had offered. Before she could continue, he threw up his hands and signaled enough. He was satisfied he had fulfilled his responsibilities as a friend and was content to live and let live. He feigned a smile in order to change the mood. "O.K. I have one more question. Tell me whether he's a son of a bitch or not."

Nedra was taken back by my remark and wasn't quite sure how to reply. "Is he a what? Batman, what the hell are you talking about?"

"Is he a son of a bitch? You know, a guy who makes love with a four inch screw driver and then kisses you goodbye with an eight inch tongue." As soon as it left his mouth, he bolted for the door. Laughing wildly, she jumped out of the bed and ran behind him, beating him in the back with her pillow.

CHAPTER 7

Batman's conversation with Nedra set him back a half-hour. His routine was to make it to the gym five to ten minutes prior to it opening. He would spend the time horsing around with the guys. It also afforded him an opportunity to get loose and play in the first game. By the time he made it, the guys were well into the hustle game. The way it worked was that whoever won the hustle automatically became the captain of the first team to play. After that, everyone lined up to shoot for who would choose the second based on score. He had been playing at Allen Park gymnasium since moving to Miami and knew all the guys fairly well. Depending on who won the hustle and who picked the second team, he could pretty much count on being picked up.

The first person he spotted was Shaggy. Being his best friend, he knew he would save him a spot if he won. He walked to the edge of the court. Shag saw him and greeted him saying, "What's up, Batman?"

"It's all good," Batman replied casually. "What's up with you?"

Shag looked at him and laughed. "I'm pimpin' 'em hard, my brotha."

Batman knew exactly what he'd referred to. Shag considered himself a ladies man and took great pride in his promiscuous life style. Having grown up with him, Batman thought it was the funniest thing. As kids, Shag never had any girlfriends. All the girls would tease him about his looks and dress. However, as an adult, he seemed to be making up for lost time.

Batman asked, "By the way, what happened with you last night. I came looking for you and you were gone."

"I'll tell you about it later. Right now, I'm trying to loosen up my knees. They're killing me."

Batman moved his hand to his mouth and made a "V" and jokingly said, "If you stayed off of them, they wouldn't hurt so bad."

Everyone laughed. "Look who's talking," Shag rebutted. "You just be careful when you get out here, cause if someone hits you in the mouth, it will ruin your sex life."

Batman slid off his warm-up bottoms and stepped into the lane where a pack of guys were huddled and jockeying for a rebound.

"What's the high score?" he asked.

Aaron, another regular, replied, "Nineteen. You came just in time for me to end it." He got the rebound then added, "I could have ended it long ago, but I wanted you to get here to see how it's done." He took the ball out to the top of the key with Batman guarding him.

"I'm here now so let me see you end so we can get a real game cranked up." Batman hand checked him and chided, "Don't be scared. It's just a little defense I'm putting on you. If you're scared, call the police."

Everyone laughed as Aaron attempted to get by Batman. Batman continued to hand check and push him until Batman finally kicked the ball off his foot.

Aaron laughed. "Batman, you ain't nothing but a hack."

Their horse play lasted another couple of minutes before Aaron eventually won. Batman managed to put in a couple of shots, but was still nowhere near the leading scorer. Another brother ended up picking second.

"Hey, let me and my homeboy run with you," Shag said.

Trying to get the point across while sounding arrogant, Batman chimed in, "If you want to win, you'd best listen to my man and do the right thing. Anyway, you owe us. We always pick you up when we choose teams."

At the same time, everyone else in the gym requested they get picked up. After a small amount of convincing, Shag and Batman were selected as fourth and fifth picks. Walking onto the court, each team member matched up with a man from the other team. Batman recognized the guy he would be playing against and said, "Brother, do yourself a favor and hold someone else. If you don't, I'm gonna do things to you that I wouldn't wish on my worst enemy."

Everyone knew Batman was a talker and generally ignored him. The guy he would be playing was a good player whom he had gone up against in the past. Generally, he had his days, and Batman had his.

Batman's team got the first ball, and Shag passed it in to him.

"Don't worry about Batman, because I'm checking him," his defensive man said.

Batman dribbled and pointed at what looked like a six-year-old girl seated in the bleachers. "You can't check that little girl's homework, how are you going to check me? I came to ball today."

"We'll see what you say after the game. I'm putting you in lockdown," he replied.

The game went back and forth, but Batman's team ultimately won. The first game was always the hardest. After that, Batman's team won three more games before finally losing. He wasn't too disappointed, considering he had become quite tired. He grabbed his warm-ups and headed to the bleacher position where Shag had placed his bag. Once there, he sat down to chat and catch his breath.

"Now, as I asked earlier," he said. "What happened to you last night? You were gone when I came looking."

Seemingly dejected, Shag replied, "Oh nothing much. I picked up a girl from Overtown and took her home."

It was unlike Shag lack enthusiam about his exploits, especially when he was able to score on the first night. It was as if he kept a scorecard or something. Depending on how much money he spent and how long it took him to have sex with her, his score went up or down.

Somewhat reluctant, Batman replied, "Oh yeah. Go ahead then. How was she?"

Shag shook his head. "I've had better and I've had worse. It was all right. No big deal."

Shag was a friend, but Batman had no desire to push for the complete story. He had heard enough to write a book already. "I hear you."

Both sat and watched the game. The team that had beaten them was in a tight game. A lot of fouls were being called, and it seemed like the game would last forever. On each trip down the court, someone had to be separated from fighting. Batman thought that was the worse part about basketball. You couldn't go to the court and shoot without somebody wanting to fight. His mind drifted to how he would spend the rest of the evening when Shag broke in as if he'd forgotten something.

"Batman, guess what?" he asked, shaking his head.

"What?"

"I was doing ole girl and guess what happened?"

"I don't know. What happened?" Batman said, frustrated.

"Batman, you're not going to believe this."

"I know I'm not going to believe it if you don't tell it to me," he said impatiently.

"I mean it freaked me out. I was doing ole girl, and I slipped out of her right into her butt hole."

"Say what?" he exclaimed. He gave it a second to sink in. "Did you stop?"

Shag hesitated and then replied casually, "Naw, I kept on. She didn't say anything, so I didn't say anything. I came right in her behind."

Astonished, Batman looked at Shag in bewilderment. He was trying to conceptualize just what he had told him. "Damn, Shag, I know you didn't do that."

"Why, what do you think?"

Batman couldn't believe Shag asked him what he thought. "It's not what I think, but what I know. You must have picked up a sure enough freak. I keep telling you brothas these women are freaks. Every brotha wants to think he's the Mac Man. Every brotha has to be all that and a bag of chips. It's not that we're all that. It's that they're whores. It's what the police call modus operandi. The girls we pick up, we're not the first to leave the club with them, take them home and have sex with them. Don't you know they've already crossed that line? That's why they're comfortable with it. It's their mode of operation."

Batman stopped to allow Shag time to absorb his comments.

"God bless you, brotha, cause you're a better man than me. I would have stopped and asked that freak what's wrong with her."

Shag looked scared. He rubbed over his head with his hands. "You don't think she had something do you?"

Batman could have jumped out of my seat. What he was saying couldn't have been any clearer. He stared him down. "Shag, please don't tell me you jumped in the pool without a swim suit. Look at me and tell me you weren't skinny-dipping. Man, you know that Ninja is out there. That's why I give you those condoms that Nedra brings from work. If you get the Big Ninja, it's over."

"Hey, I know. That's why I'm telling you. I knew I had messed up as soon as I did it," he said exasperated. "You think Nedra can help a brotha out?"

"You mean can she give you a test?" Batman answered, regaining his composure. "I don't see why not. She keeps her stuff with her everywhere she goes. She should be able to do it without you going down there. Let me ask her and get back to you. In the mean time, you'd better use a raincoat when you pick up those freaks. Especially when they come from Big Daddy's. The majority of the chicks that come there are from the Pork and Bean projects over on Northeast 2nd. Nedra told me about the Pork and Beans. The Ninja is infecting people over there like nobody's business."

Content Shag had gotten the message, Batman lightened up and asked, "Hey, you see the girl I was dancing with?"

"You mean the one that looked like Vivica Fox with the short doo?"

"You mean Halle Berry," Batman said, correcting him. "I was sure hoping to get with her. You know her?"

"Nope. Weren't you able to get something to follow up with?"

"Brotha, she wasn't giving up nothing. She never gave me a chance. Said she was married."

Shag smiled and got up to leave. "So what, you're not jealous."

"No but her old man is," he replied, using the line they'd given him.

Shag grabbed his bag to go. "I'm outta here. Pimp 'em hard, homeboy."

CHAPTER 8

Andrea Rivera sat in her office, idly reviewing the stack of grievance cases that covered her desk. For her, Monday's were the worst. She had been an EEO counselor for twelve years and had long passed burned out, the last six having been a battle of attrition. The depression of being in a dead end position compounded with the stress related to the nature of the work taking its toll. She had entertained a career move into the private sector, but was too close to being vested in the state retirement system. There was no way she would walk away with nothing to show for her grief.

Through the grapevine, it had come to her attention that a supervisory opening would be coming available in her section. With her education and experience, she was sure to be a leading candidate. Such a promotion would not only afford her an opportunity to do something different, but result in a much needed pay raise. The word was she and three others were the leading candidates for the position. Due to the competitive nature of the position, she surmised that the annual evaluation of each candidate would weigh heavily in the selection process.

She flipped through her calendar and concluded that her evaluation was less than three weeks away. The thought of an evaluation under such circumstances made her cringe. EEO counselors worked under very strict timelines. They had thirty days in which to complete the counseling process. That was the bad news. The good news was that their supervisors were just as overwork. Most, if not all, of her previous evaluations reflected her knowledge of the process more so than her performance. However, with a promotion at stake, she could not depend on the trend holding. An accurate evaluation of her current caseload would conclude that she had failed to issue notice of timely review or even worse had made inadequate attempts to informally resolve allegations. Not willing to concede the position, she resolved that she had three weeks to shore up her performance.

Without a thorough review, she surmised that at least three of the cases had exceeded federal guidelines for achieving resolution. She stared into nowhere and thought to herself how unfair it was to be held accountable when everyone was aware her caseload far exceeded recommended guidelines. However, knowing her supervisor, accountable she would be. He would have no problem using it to keep her from getting the position. Realizing the futility of her situation, she searched her memory for any potential means by which to short circuit the traditional process. Drastic times called for drastic measures, and the time had come for these cases to be closed.

Andrea sat up in her chair, retrieved the files of the three that she thought had exceeded their closing dates and separated them from the others. Included in each file were statements from the aggrieved, their witnesses, and their supervisor. Additional information obtained from the human resources department was included to shed light on the complaint. She placed each file on her desk and reviewed the in-take form to determine the basis of their complaint. The Civil Rights Act of 1964 provided five categories under which an aggrieved party could file a complaint: race, religion, national origin, sex and most recently as a result of an amendment, age. The law required the complainant provide a basis and an issue. The basis of the first two cases were sex. In each, the respective supervisors had allegedly demanded sex as a criteria for promotion. Aside from race, sex was the most common basis alleged by aggrieved parties. Quickly reading her notes, she decided there were questions of fact and law that would have to be resolved. Shaking her head, she concluded they would need more detailed attention.

Frustrated at the thought of not being able to resolve the previous two quickly, she retrieved the final case. The grounds for the complaint was racial discrimination. The aggrieved party was a young black male in the department of sanitation who alleged he was denied promotion due to his race. During their initial discussion, she had suggested employee assistance as a means of resolving his dispute. He had rejected it and chosen instead to pursue an administrative judgment. He had provided in his in-take interview that the only remedy he was willing to consider was promotion to, as he put it, dipsy-dumpster driver. Andrea almost laughed when she considered that her long overdue promotion could be held up by a person whose purpose in life was to be a dipsy-dumpster driver.

After a further review, Andrea decided the information in his statement was extremely weak. He had supplied no substantive evidence that he had been discriminated against and had provided no witnesses to collaborate his claims. On the other hand, she had interviewed his supervisor, the responsible management official, and he had provided a cache of documents supporting why the claimant wasn't promoted. Included were time records that showed the claimant to be late as many as four days out of five. Also, there were signed statements from the driver of his truck that he was insubordinate and hostile to supervisory direction. In her time as a counselor, Andrea had seen and heard more than her share of frivolous cases. Her take on this case was that the most appropriate action would have been for the claimant to have been fired long ago. However, clearly marked in the top right hand portion of the in-take form under the line union status was "active member." As a union member, she knew firing the claimant was virtually impossible under any circumstances short of mass murder.

Complicating the issue further was the data she had received from the human resources department. Although the claimant could not prove he had been discriminated against, a prudent person analyzing the number of African-Americans serving as drivers in the sanitation department could allege a deeper problem. This problem dealt not with one individual but with an entire class. Although the promotion policies were facially neutral, it could be demonstrated that there was disparate impact. It was a classic case of effect versus intent. The aggrieved had a snowball's chance in hell of proving intent, however the effect was as plain as day.

Based on the claimants desired remedy, it was unlikely he would accept her decision if it was unfavorable. That meant the case would go forward and could end up as high as the Washington D.C. office. If it fell into the wrong hands, the entire department would be placed under intense scrutiny. The department, as was all in Miami, was run by Cubans. Being Cuban, she knew they would be adverse to any settlement that resulted in Blacks being placed in positions predominantly occupied with her fellow Cuban brethren. With racial tensions running as high as they were, the last thing she needed was to be stuck in the middle of a long drawn out battle.

The only quick resolution she saw was to offer the complainant an alternative. She could first attempt to hard ball him into accepting nothing. If this didn't work, she could reserve an alternate option.

She picked up the telephone and called an old acquaintance in the department of public works. She smiled when she thought of her ingenuity. On a few occasions, she'd worked under the table to dispose of sexual harassment charges against him. The last was an open and shut case, which could have resulted in his dismissal. An immigrant female from Colombia who had accepted a position cleaning the building had filed it. One evening, while working late, she had alleged he had forced her to have sex with him under the pretense that she would be dismissed if she didn't. Her evidence, combined with his previous record, was daunting. However, Andrea had convinced her that to go forward would jeopardize her work status. Unhappy, but unwilling to risk being sent back to Colombia, she had retracted the charges against him. In return, he had graciously offered to return the favor if Andrea ever needed his assistance. She used her shoulder to hold the telephone to her right ear as she dialed the number while simultaneously retrieving a settlement form.

It took three rings for someone on the other end to answer. What sounded like an African-American female answered saying, "Good morning. Dade County Department of Public Works. May I help you?"

Impressed at her professionalism, Andrea jubilantly replied, "Good morning to you. Is Louis Rodriguez available?"

"Please hold." Within seconds, she was back on the line. "Please hold while I transfer you."

Andrea smiled to herself over her good fortune. It always helped knowing people in high places. She had scratched Louis's back, and now he was about to take care of an itch she had.

The voice of a Cuban male came on the line just in time to interrupt her thoughts. "Louis Rodriguez, may I help you?"

"Louis, Andrea Rivera from EEO."

Louis's heart began to race. He and Andrea had talked frequently on the telephone, but only when he had managed to get into trouble. He wondered who could be complaining now. He had pretty much been on his best behavior, aside from a few dirty jokes. And as far as sex, his latest escapade was purely consensual. He had even had her sign a statement saying such in case she decided to pursue charges against him later.

"Andrea, how's it going?"

Andrea heard the nervousness in his voice. She smiled, thinking he probably had someone in his office as he spoke. She was tempted to string him along, but decided her time was more valuable.

"Louis, don't worry, you haven't done anything. At least not anything that's been reported," she said sarcastically. "I'm calling on another matter. I have a young man I need to move. I would like to offer him at least a level 7 position. What can you help me out with?"

Louis knew very well what was being asked. He owed Andrea for saving his hide and now she was collecting. He was all prepared to go along with it. He thought it was the least he could do. However, Louis loved women, and Andrea had always intrigued him. Why not help her and help himself at the same time, he thought.

"Right now I'm not aware of what exactly we have open," he said slyly. "Why don't you let me check and say maybe we get together for drinks, and I tell you then?"

Had the offer come from someone with an ounce of morals, Andrea would have been flattered. But she knew Louis and had no desire what-so-ever to have drinks with him or anything else.

Slightly offended, she replied indignantly, "No Louis. I have a better idea. How about I reinstate that last case and then meet you for coffee in the unemployment line?"

Louis knew she meant business. Anyone who would convince an abused woman to retract her allegations was not to be messed with. As professionally as he could manage, he replied, "That won't be necessary. What exactly do you have in mind? We have openings on the meter crew all the time. They're level 6 with promotional potential to level 7."

"What else do you have? Anything driving a truck or something?"

Louis thought to himself. "Well, we have backhoes. But they're level 8 and are usually reserved for the brethren. They operate the trench machines needed to lay out the sewer system."

Andrea would have settled for the road meter crew. She knew Louis would have a hard time explaining how a black man with no experience could be brought in and placed on a backhoe over Cubans. However, insulted by his come on, she felt obliged to make him suffer. Without hesitating, she responded, "That'll do. I'll speak with him and send him over. I'm sure he'll enjoy being the only black on the road crew."

Louis wanted to resist but didn't have the nerve. "O.K.," he quietly replied,

Andrea hung up the telephone and stamped closed on the outside of the folder. She rose and walked around the desk then placed it on top of her file. On her way back to her seat, the telephone rang. She reached across the front of the desk to retrieve it. "Hello."

"Ms. Rivera, there's a man out here to see you."

She recognized the voice as the black female receptionist. Although Cubans occupied the majority of the professional positions, the lower level administrative support positions were predominantly staffed with African-Americans. This was particularly important when it came to analyzing hiring practices. In isolation, it would seem Cubans and whites were the only people being hired for better paying jobs. In essence, it was true, however, by including the janitorial, cafeteria and other lower level, they were able to alter the numbers quite considerably. The department provided combined numbers during presentations to defend hiring practices.

Andrea checked her watch. "Send him in please." She rushed to her chair to put on her game face. She considered counseling to be akin to negotiating. As a rule, she always attempted to be pessimistic during the sessions. This way, the aggrieved would be more likely to settle for the first offer. Hearing the knock on the door, she replied, "Come in."

Without rising, she continued, "Good morning. I'm Andrea Rivera. I've been assigned your case. Please, have a seat."

The first thing Batman noticed was her perfume. He was a stickler for perfume. Having hung in bars a large part of his life, he'd come to realize just how hard it was to get the right amount for the desired effect. Andrea's was light enough to barely notice but heavy enough to distinguish her from anyone else. Her perfume scent matched her body scent to perfection. Batman smiled and commented, "Nice perfume."

"Thank you." Without further small talk she said, "We need to review your case and attempt to reach a settlement. I've reviewed your written statements and spoke with your supervisor. First, I'd like to make sure all the information on your in-take form is correct." She took the form off her desk. "Your name please?"

As he always did, he replied, "Batman."

"I'm sorry. I need your given name."

"Batman is my given name. It was given to me by my mother."

His mother had given him the nickname years earlier, and based on his outlook toward life, it had stuck. She had come into his room to find his bed broken at the head. This caused the head to be lower than the foot. Unfazed, he had climbed in and slept quite comfortably. When asked how long it had been that way, he informed her weeks. Angry, she had commented that he was the laziest most trifling child she had ever seen. The fact that he would rather sleep upside down like a bat, rather than put something under the springs to make the bed level, compelled her to call him batman.

Years later there was an incident where she loaned him her car for what would be the last time. Returning from a date, he decided to get high. Once home he parked the car, forgetting to take a half-smoked joint out of the ashtray. The next morning she discovered it before leaving for work. Lucky for him he was forewarned by the screams and shouts from outside all the way to his bedroom door. Within seconds, his door flew open with her standing there angry as all get out. Holding up the joint as if passing it to him, she hollered, "Batman!!!" He knew he was in serious trouble but tried to play it off.

Looking innocent, he calmly stated, "You go ahead, I don't do that." From that time on, whenever he got into trouble, she referred to him as Batman.

"I'm sorry, but I need to know the name on your birth certificate."

"Oh, that would be Carter Osborne," he answered hesitantly.

"Thank you Mr. Osborne."

"No problem. Your wish is my command," he replied politely.

What Andrea really wished was that he'd just go away. She smiled slightly and tried to appear impartial. "As I said earlier, I've reviewed your information and your supervisor's information. From what I can see, your supervisor provides good evidence that not only were you not discriminated against, but that you were actually treated quite fairly in that you weren't fired. Mr. Gonzales along with your direct supervisor have signed statements saying that you were more often late than on time."

After finishing, Andrea waited for a comment. However, he seemed indifferent to what she had said. She sensed there would be no reply and asked, "What time does your shift start? And what time does it end?"

"It starts when I get there," he answered, pausing a few seconds before adding, "and it ends when I leave." Batman's tone and delivery were reflective of his indifference. He had gone through this more often than he could count with Gonzales and was merely restating versus defending his position.

The look on Andrea's face turned from objective to hostile. Although she said nothing, he could see he had given the wrong answer. Whatever her impression of him, it was falling fast. He was in no mood to go to battle with the EEO counselor.

Batman figured he'd better try to diffuse the situation while maintaining his cool exterior. He calmly said, "Look, I'm not trying to be hard, but believe me I'm not the problem. I know you're doing your job. But regardless of what your rules say, I'm not going to allow anyone to treat me like crap, and that's what they are trying to do over there. I'm willing to take this as far as it needs to go. You told me what Gonzales had to say about me. Now I'm going to tell you about him. No offense, but he's one nasty, rotten Cuban. He has no management skills, and he ain't trying to get any. To make matters worst, he has no desire to see a black man move up. I'm not talking about taking his job but about driving a damn garbage truck. And what's worse is he's mean to the core. He wouldn't give a cripple crab a crutch if he had a whole lumber yard and all it needed was a splinter."

Andrea listened as he spoke. She knew he was right in his personal assessment of Gonzales. She had felt the same way when speaking with him. What he had not mentioned was that not only did he not like Blacks, but also women. Gonzales had a narrow view of the world that had come from people allowing him to push them around. Right now, she admired the fact that Batman was unwilling to take any crap off Gonzales.

"Look, Mr. Osborne. This is what we have. You say you've been discriminated against. He says you should be fired. We're at an impasse. Me, I'm just a lowly counselor, looking for a way to fix this whole mess where everyone is satisfied." She leaned forward in her chair to make eye contact. "I have a proposition if you're interested in hearing it."

Batman immediately perked up and became more attentive. He was looking for a way out, and if she had one, the least he could do was listen. "Sure, let's hear it."

Andrea knew she had him before she even began. The key was to get him interested and then seem like he was getting much better than he could have gotten if the case were to go forward. She picked up a pen and used it to instruct. "O.K., it works like this. I move you out of the garbage department to another department. Gonzales gets rid of you. You get another better paying position."

Growing up in Mississippi, Batman had been taught to beware of white folks, or in this case, Cubans bearing gifts. He was anxious to get the matter settled. However, he was not about to agree to anything without hearing all the details. He sat straight in his chair and spoke somewhat hesitantly. "First, exactly where will I be working, and second, what will I be doing there?"

"What I have in mind is that you be transferred over to the water department. Once there, you'll operate a backhoe. I'm not exactly sure of the official title of the position, but it's a pay grade eight. That's at least seven thousand dollars more than you make now."

Batman realized this could be a trap to get him to move to a place where he'd be dismissed for some bogus reason. "And how do I know when I get over there that I won't have to work with a clown like Gonzales?"

Andrea had hoped he would ask this question. That way it would make it seem as though she had given more thought to her proposal than she really had. Smiling, she replied, "Don't worry. I know the manager over there. He has his issues, but believe me, race isn't one of them."

Batman waited a minute to digest her proposal. It seemed to him like the natural thing to do was to accept. However, he didn't want too move to fast and regret it later. After considering his options, he leaned forward and extended his hand across her desk. "I think we've got a deal."

She joined him in smiling. She received his handshake and replied, "A deal it is."

Another satisfied customer, he thought.

CHAPTER 9

Batman walked out of the human resources building, thanking God for his good fortune. After accepting the transfer, he had been required to sign a stack of forms. Andrea had requested he write a letter of reassignment to Gonzales, thanking him for the opportunity to work there. In return, Gonzales would write a letter supporting his transfer with promotion to the water department. Batman also had to agree to accept the transfer as final settlement of any claim and not to seek to reinstate the case later. For this, he received assurance that the garbage department would remove all unfavorable documents from his official personnel file and adjust his evaluation scores to reflect "fully successful." He smiled to himself as he imaged having his "F"s changed to "A"s. He laughed aloud when he thought about how angry Gonzales would be when Andrea told him he would actually be helping Batman to a new higher paying position. No doubt, Gonzales would rant and rave. However, in the short time Batman had known Andrea, he had become impressed with how she handled her business. As such, knew that she would ultimately get Gonzales to see the light. More than likely, she would lie and say if the case went before a judge, he would lose and it could lead to a dismantling of Cuban cronyism in the department.

Against Andrea's wishes, Batman insisted on making one last stop by the yard to say goodbye to the guys. Andrea had advised that he was not to divulge any of the terms of his transfer. The limit of what he could offer was that he had found a new position and was reporting immediately. This handicapped him from getting the full enjoyment of walking out on top. However, he understood her position; if an appearance that he had used the system to get a promotion surfaced, the department would be deluged with grievances.

By the time Batman made it to the Gator, his stomach was growling something fierce. He thought that if he didn't get something in it soon, it would attack his intestines. He checked his watch and realized he was running late of his usual lunch. He'd only had a glass of OJ that morning and was feeling the effects by way of a slight headache. He scanned his memory for what eateries were in the area and came to a decision to try Jerry's on 27th.

He pulled into the parking lot right as the lunch crowd was clearing out. Family owned and operated, Jerry's was the *crème de la crème* of soul food eating in Miami. The food was par excellent, and the black citizenry who ate there ranged from politicians, to athletes, to professionals, to community leaders and down to the lowest level street thugs and drug dealers. For him, it was, and had been, at the top of his eating spots for the entirety of his stay in Miami. It provided him that down home meal when he was unable to go home. The only complaint was that the food was heavy.

It reminded him of the joke about the rich white family that employed a maid of such fair complexion that they could not tell her race. The lady of the house was well pleased with the maid's work but was quite intrigued by her inability to distinguish. Day after day, she would invite her friends over to meet the maid then afterwards secretly guess her race. As fate would have it, one day after having a close associate meet the maid, the lady of the house was offered a solution. She was directed to have the maid fix a large meal for lunch and then invite her to participate. If afterwards she asked for coffee, she was definitely white. On the other hand, if afterwards she stole away for a nap... Suffice it to say, Jerry's served the type meals that distinguished blacks from whites. It was a good place to avoid if you had afternoon meetings.

The sitting area was small by any standards. A back wall had recently been knocked down to provide additional room for diners. An old-fashioned counter ran the entire length of the back wall. Bar stools were interspersed throughout the length of the counter. Eight tables, each surrounded by four small chairs, sat in the middle of the floor. The tables were no larger than card tables, and the chairs appeared so frail as not to be capable of sustaining the weight of some of the XXL patrons who ate there. On the front wall, near the large plate glass window, were three eating booths. Each booth was capable of seating four people.

There were only ten to fifteen people left eating, so Batman had his choice of seats. He knew and was friendly with the entire staff. Prior to taking his seat, he poked his head through the food delivery window and shouted greetings to the back. A reply from several voices came quickly. It wasn't long before Gail, his server, came to take his order. She and he had a good-natured feud in which they teased each other.

She allowed him to get comfortable in his seat as she approached with a huge smile on her face. She looked old enough to have been his mother and on occasion had tried to handle him as such.

"Well if it isn't batboy in his custom made bat mobile." Confident she had gotten the attention of the other diners, she asked, "How's life in the garbage business these days?" She hesitated long enough to laugh at her own joke. "I'm not one to be nosy, but just how in the hell can a Negro who just got to town on a watermelon truck and working on the back of a garbage truck afford a Lincoln Navigator?"

The entire room fell out laughing. The staff knew him and knew where he worked. The patrons had seen him pull up and may have wondered. Regardless, she had made a public offering of his employment status that had managed to make him the butt of her humor. Gail's humor was one of the reasons many people continued to return. Her motto was "I kid because I care."

Batman knew that if he didn't stop her momentum before she got up a head of steam, he could forget eating his meal in peace. His only recourse was to embarrass her back into the kitchen. He laughed with everyone and waited for the room to quiet. Sensing he had everyone's attention, he said, "On the first count you're right and you're wrong. I may have just gotten here on a watermelon truck, but don't fool yourself, cause I was driving. I wasn't back there with the melons." He felt the crowd lighten. "As far as how I can afford a Navigator from the back of a garbage truck, well it's no secret. I'm the fat whore pimp. I pimp fat whores like yourself, take the money and pay my car note."

A big "whoooo" arose from the room. A few shouts of "Oh no, he didn't," rang out from the back.

He knew Gail's weight was her sore spot. She had probably been on every diet known to man. However, the effect, if any, was unnoticeable. Normally he wouldn't have used her weight as an issue, but he was running low in new material and wasn't feeling very creative at the time.

Pleased, Batman looked around at his audience. "What can I say. Pimpin' ain't dead, the women just scurd," he said, using his best ghetto dialect. "That's why I have to pimp big whores."

Gail couldn't believe he'd go below the belt. He saw beads of sweat forming on her forehead and knew she was about to come with it. Talking over the crowd, she replied, "What you mean is you're the gay pimp. I know I saw you somewhere recently but couldn't put my finger on it. It was down on Biscayne and 10th selling booty to those fags."

The crowd let out a roar. Gail and Batman had moved from shadow boxing to a full-fledged street brawl. Batman was indifferent to her reference and was tempted to let it go. If it had stopped then, it would have been a draw. However, since she drew first blood, he decided he'd throw one last punch to see if he could knock her out.

Showing no ill effects from her comments, he replied, "Now, Gail, why would you say such a thing. You know we go way back. Why I knew you back when you could walk through a door without turning sideways. Now look at you. Why you acting like we don't know each other."

The crowd fell out. She shot him a look of disapproval. He, in return, smiled his apology and mouthed, "I kid because I care."

She attempted to make a graceful exit. "You're lucky I got work to do. Now give me your order before we be here all day."

As much as he liked Gail, he didn't know if she was beyond spitting in his food. Therefore, he ordered off the line. His meal of smothered pork chops, mash potatoes, turnip bottoms and corn bread came right out. Gail set it in front of him then headed back to get him a sweet tea.

"You want desert while I'm back there? Cause I'm not gone be running back and forth for you all day, Mr. Big Whore Pimp."

While waiting for his order, he surveyed the crowd. One person he recognized, who was not a regular, was Joe Nathan Creel. He had played professional basketball for at least ten years. Now, however, he was just like everyone else. Doing what he could to try and catch a break. He had made millions of dollars, but had also lost much of it. Batman looked at him and wondered if he ever considered the hundred of thousands of dollars he basically gave away in fines and suspensions. During his career, like many of the other professional black athletes, he had been fined for everything from arriving late to practice, behavior detrimental to the team, smoking pot, you name it. Many had come from poor families and poor neighborhoods. However, they acted as if they had forgotten where they came from and were now willing to squander the opportunity to keep twenty-five to fifty thousand dollars.

The sad part was, Batman mused, as Black men, they didn't realize the window of opportunity that had been presented them. They had hit the jackpot and started acting like they were entitled or even worse white. In Batman's opinion, Whites enjoyed a door of opportunity. But for Blacks, the window of opportunity was just that. Of the three hundred and sixty-five days in a year, the door to a house opens just about every one of them. The same can't be said for the window. During the summer, it's so hot out the air is on, so the windows are closed to keep cool. During the winter, it's so cold out the heat is on, thus the windows are closed to keep warm. It's only when the environment outside is perfect that the window is open. And for Blacks, he felt the environment must be perfect to be afforded access to the opportunities that others enjoyed on a daily basis. He believed this more so for athletes. For him there were no other positions that would offer them a comparable salary for comparable skills. However, he Continually watched them forfeiting the chance to take advantage of it.

Gail, not being one to hold a grudge, returned and asked if he cared for dessert with his meal. He turned his thoughts from Joe Nathan and answered, "I'll pass. You've been so sweet, I think I can do without any more sugar today."

By the time he had gotten into his meal, the diner was all but empty. He sat eating silently while contemplating the events of the morning. In between thoughts, he looked out the window and noted of the passing cars. This was a habit of his that Nedra often criticized. He looked into cars to view the female drivers. He had even managed to stop a chick or two and gotten a date. On this day, across from where he was seated, stopped at the traffic light was a red Jeep Cherokee. The first person he saw was the young woman behind the steering wheel. She had an island look and wore braided extensions. Her heavy makeup was the first thing he noticed. She couldn't have been any more than thirty. He concluded she was reasonably attractive and shifted his gaze to the passenger seat. In the passenger seat with a big smile on his face sat a black male with a low-cut fade. Almost immediately, he recognized the man and did a double take. Using his telescopic sights, he locked in on him. *That looks like Brian.* The light turned green, and the Jeep continued down 27th. As it passed, he tried to get a better look.

He managed to get a glancing side look. *No, that's not him.*

Evidently, Brian had become a part of his reticular memory. Reticular memory was a term he'd learned from watching the discovery channel. It's like when a woman buys a dress she really likes. She wears the dress and notices everyone else with a dress just like it. It's not that everyone went out and bought one because she did. It's just that now that she owned one, her memory was more sensitive to recognizing it when in the presence of someone wearing one like it. He sighed from the stress of a long day. Now that he had met Brian, his memory would probably be activated whenever he saw him or anyone who looked like him.

"See somebody you know?" Gail asked.

"Sure, looked like a friend of mine."

"A *girlfriend*, I hope," Gail said.

"A friend, friend. And if you don't start nothing, it won't be nothing," he replied, laughing.

CHAPTER 10

After leaving Jerry's, Batman returned to the yard to retrieve his gear and say goodbye to the crew. He was almost wistful as he entered for what he knew would be the last time. Regardless of how things worked out at the water department, he had no intention of returning. That he had stayed as long as he had was a testament to his contrariness more so than his character. He had allowed himself to become entangled in a pissing contest with Gonzales and Emerson that had resulted in him staying out of spite rather than gain. However, his feelings for them prevented him from even considering anything better. This was where they belonged and where they would be. Therefore, his staying for the wrong reasons had really hurt him more than them.

Abdullah and Pedro had finished cleaning the truck and were loitering in the yard. Both had yet to change out of their work clothes, so Batman assumed they were waiting for Emerson to give the word they could leave. Abdullah, as always, was laid up against the back rear wheel wield, reading literature. Batman didn't have to guess the subject matter. It was probably on the plight of Black America and how black men had been brained washed into accepting the lifestyle of the oppressor. *God bless him,* Batman thought, *when so many people are willing to accept whatever is told to them, at least he's attempting to educate himself on the real issues.* Not far from where Abdullah stood reading, Pedro stood in a circle with four others, chatting idly.

Batman saw them before they saw him and realized he would miss them. Working on the back of a garbage truck wasn't pretty. The stench of garbage, along with people complaining their can wasn't placed where it should have been, was enough to sour anyone on the work. However, if there was one thing it did was give Batman, it was humility. Humility can't be bought, stolen or faked. Humility allowed him to look at people and see past their faults. It allowed him to accept people not because of, but in spite of.

Batman greeted them as he approached. "Pedro, Abdullah, what's up cats?"

Pedro turned from his previous conversation and replied in broken English, "Hello, *amigo*. The U-yon take care of yo job, no?"

Everyone broke out laughing, even Abdullah. He closed his book on his finger and nodded his acknowledgement.

Smiling, Batman replied, "It's all good, Pedro. What about you? What are you all doing hanging around so long?"

"Dey say you no longer with us. We wait to see who come wit us next."

Batman laughed outright. "Well they say right this time. I'm out of here. I got a new job and a new attitude. I stopped by to get my gear and say goodbye."

Abdullah heard he was leaving and extended his hand. Although divided in their personal beliefs, they were united in the mutual plight visited upon black men. Batman took it and stepped to him so they could go breast to breast.

"Take care of yourself. Follow Allah and truth," Abdullah said. "I knew you would be leaving soon. You never belonged here. Allah only brought you here to teach you. But now you must go to fulfill your true calling."

"Thanks," Batman replied jokingly. "I pray all goes well with you, too. But all the same, right now I'm stuck on following long legs and dead Presidents."

After Abdullah, Pedro stepped forward and gave him a hug. "All is well, no?" he asked.

Batman looked him in the eye. "All is well, Pedro. And all will be better as soon as I see Gonzales and get my walking papers."

Pedro stepped back and looked at Batman with genuine concern. Andrea had advised Batman say nothing or as little as possible about his transfer. He was intent on following her advice. "Look, it's all good. Don't worry about me. They gave me something better. And as soon as I get settled in, I want you all to come with me. I'm going to the water department to mess with them for awhile."

Batman shook the other guys' hands and walked off for the office. He still needed a copy of his transfer package. That meant he would have to see Gonzales. When he walked into the main office, Gonzales was waiting for him.

"You come for ya papers, I assume," Gonzales stated.

"Yes sir, yes sir, three bags full," Batman said. "And once I get them, I'm on to the next town to shoot the next Sheriff."

"Berry good. I glad to see you go. It's betta for me and betta for you."

"Yes sir, yes sir, three bags full."

Gonzales handed him the package. "Osborne, you nevva belong here. Ders nothin worse dan a man bein somewhere he don't belong. I'm glad yu go. If not, one of us would be in trouble."

Batman held his stare. "The one of us would have been the one who can't speak English." He was tempted to say something contrary in order to provoke him one last time. He wanted to be careful not to blow the deal but couldn't resist the temptation. "Gonzales, every twenty-four hours the world turns over. Somebody on the top is on the bottom, and somebody on the bottom is on the top. The key is hanging in there until your twenty-four comes. It may be naïve to consider the water department as the top, but coming from working in stench for a lousy clown like you, I would argue differently."

Finished, he took the package and left without further conversation. He walked outside, thinking that was the second time in less than five minutes that someone had told him he didn't belong there. Maybe everyone else saw something he didn't see. Whatever the case, he resolved to give his situation some thought. After having endured the constant antagonism of having worked there, the last thing he needed was to go to the water department when as they said, he didn't belong there.

He reentered the yard in time to see Emerson. His look told Batman he knew the full details of his transfer. Emerson followed him with his eyes, and when he was sure Batman was looking, he spat on the ground in his direction. The thought crossed Batman's mind to walk over and call him the N-word. However, his opinion of him was so low that it would have been a compliment. *God bless him,* he thought and kept on walking.

CHAPTER 11

Nedra sat under her hair dryer, reading the latest edition of her favorite magazine. The lead article read "What Black Men Really Want From Black Women." What caught her attention was that although the question was what black men would like from black women, the picture accompanying the title line was of a black man romancing a white woman. The thesis of the article was that black men desire a queen for a wife and a whore for a girlfriend. It suggested that if black women were to please black men then they would have to forsake the traditional missionary sex scenes and interject some of the more adventurous contemporary scenes described in the article. Nedra was open to some of suggested means by which more adventure could be put into the relationship, but was miffed at the suggestion that white women were more apt to go all out to please their men than black women. *This is just what black men need. Another excuse to turn to white women for comfort, but sistahs with their problems.* It had always been a peeve to her to see successful black men with white women. Where were all the white women when black men failed, or when they were locked up? They were somewhere gold digging for a more successful one. Nedra knew that Black men didn't turn to white women because of better sex, but because of low self-esteem. They saw white women as trophies, signifying they had arrived.

She closed the magazine. A part of her felt compelled to write a rebuttal to the managing editor. How dare another black female write such trash criticizing what she obviously did not understand. Sistahs got bashed from everyone else and didn't need another sistah doing it. She thought twice then decided why waste her time. This was someone else's problem now. Let those women looking for a man worry about such foolishness. She had her man and the last thing he was looking for was a white woman. Her man knew whom he was and wasn't interested in trophies. He was a man of conviction and principle, totally committed to the cause. She smiled sheepishly. *Just in case, I'll turn him out come Friday.*

Nedra turned off the dryer and took out one of the large curlers. Feeling with her hand, she deemed her hair sufficiently dry. She slid from under the dryer and pranced to the mirror to see how she had done. Since Brian had come into her life, she had done away with the braided extensions and taken to doing her hair once a week. Normally, she went to a beauty salon, but he had suggested that she was more capable of managing her beauty as professional stylists were. This was just another compliment she attributed to him—his ability to make her feel beautiful and want to go all out.

Brian had further suggested that the money she saved could be put to better use by investing in stock options. Initially, she was skeptical. Not having known him for a significant length a time, she requested to see actual returns. He willingly provided records of personal transactions made on-line using a dedicated identification number. The more she listened, the more his knowledge of investing simply amazed her. He explained to her how to read the business section to see what promising areas in which to invest. He counseled that it was never too early to start planning for retirement. Additionally, he had agreed to have a close acquaintance set her up an account that would allow her to transact her own investments. Nedra was more than excited to do so. Her head told her to relax and go slow. Her heart told her that he was planning for their future together. Agreeing, she wrote a check for an initial deposit of five hundred dollars to open her own account and agreed to make subsequent investments of five percent of her monthly gross.

As she brushed the curls from her hair, she couldn't help but think how great God really was. It was just as her Pastor had explained. Depressed about her career mobility and her lack of companionship, she had arranged to speak with him privately. She confided in him her frustration with God's plan for her life thus far. She had done all she thought required of her by God. She had even begun to tithe. However, as far as she could tell, her life was a total wreck. Not only was she alone in a far away place, but she watched as others seemingly less faithful had been blessed with soul mates. People who weren't tithing were buying new houses, new cars, and getting promotions, while she was stuck in the same old dead end situation. Her Bible said it was better to marry than to burn. She wanted to live in the will of God. She wanted to marry and have children and live in the small house with the white picket fence. She had prayed and fasted, and fasted and prayed and then fasted some more, and yet God had sent her no one.

Her pastor had listened intently and afterwards insisted that she must continue to pray and trust. He had said, "They that wait on the Lord would mount up as wings of eagles." He also counseled that in time, "God would do exceeding abundantly above all she could think or ask." Well, he was right. Just when she thought she might have to settle for the less intellectual, less polished black men left out there, her knight in shining armor had arrived to rescue her. How could she have asked for someone like him? God must have known all the time. All she needed to be was patient. She was, and now he had blessed her beyond measure. Thankful, she resolved to put in even more money beyond her tithes into church. The extra would be a reward to God for bringing her Brian.

Nedra heard the doorbell ring and wondered who it could be. She wasn't expecting anyone and decided it must have been for Batman. Not keen on the majority of his friends, she decided not to answer.

Batman knew her well enough to know that unless she was in the living room, she wouldn't answer. However, he continued to lay on the bell. He knew that sooner or later she would wonder if whoever was at the door was out of their mind. She would then be obliged to answer so she could get them told.

Batman had his keys but had intentionally rung the bell as a way of announcing himself. He felt wonderful and wanted to share it with the world. Waiting patiently, he rang and rang until he heard heavy footsteps approach the door. The pronounced sound and rhythm signaled he had succeeded in drawing her ire.

The door flew open with a rush. Nedra exclaimed, "Batman, you must be out of your good for nothing mind."

He smiled while waiting for her to ask the one the million-dollar question.

Unmoved, she asked, "Why the hell are you standing out here ringing that bell like somebody's chasing you or something?"

He remained smiling and stood silently.

"Batman, you hear me. What's wrong with you?" He could sense she was becoming truly irate, but she still hadn't asked what he was waiting for.

"Batman, I said what's wrong with you. And why are you standing there with the cat that ate the canary smile on your face?"

He let out a big sigh and grabbed her around the neck. "I thought you'd never ask. I was about to give up on you."

Nedra could see he was happy, and even though she didn't know why, her attitude became lighter. She attempted to push him away. "Batman, turn me loose." She wriggled free from his grasp. "Now tell me what you're talking about and why you come in here jumping on my neck. I ought to scream rape and have the police pick you up. I'm sure they'll be more than glad to whip your head for you."

Batman released Nedra and started Bankhead bouncing in a circle. He danced as though the music was flowing. He stopped only for a second and exclaimed, "Nedra, you're not going to believe what happened today. I don't believe it myself."

She pushed the door closed and moved to take a seat on the couch. "You're right, I'm not going to believe it, especially if you don't tell me what it is."

He changed his tone to speak properly, saying, "It, my dearest, is my position with the State of Florida, Dade County."

Nedra looked suspiciously happy. "Since you already work for them, I assume you mean you won your suit." She smiled broadly. "I know you didn't come in here and maul me because they told you that they'd let you drive a garbage truck."

Batman continued with the proper dialect. "Yea, yea and nay, my dear. Yea, I won. Yea, I'll be driving. But nay, it won't be a garbage truck." He hesitated a moment to let his comments sink in before speaking in his natural voice to say in the sincerest manner, "Nedra, I won my suit, and they're going to transfer me from the garbage department to the water department. Starting tomorrow, I'll be driving heavy equipment. I'll be using it to dig the tunnels where they lay the sewer pipes."

Nedra shot out of her seat, grabbed him around the neck and started screaming and shouting.

"Hey, wait a minute. Now who has to call the police on who?" he asked. "You're strangling me."

"Oh be quiet and give me some love."

They stood in the middle of the living room and embraced. He could smell her hair and the light scent of perfume. Her happiness for him served to make him all the more cheery.

He started to Bankhead bounce again. "Hey, how about dinner? On me."

Nedra stopped hopping around and replied seriously, "Batman, don't go spending money you haven't made yet. Why do Negroes have to spend every dime they make?"

Batman was not to be dissuaded. Today was his day, and he was going to enjoy it. "Come on. Pull up on the throttle, will you? Stop being a fogy stogie. I want to celebrate my good fortune with the lady in my life, and you're telling me to worry about tomorrow. Just who are you, my lady or my momma?"

"Neither," she stated, laughing. "And thank God I'm not, or you'd really be hearing it."

"Good, that's settled. Let's ride out to the beach. Let me throw on something and we're out of here."

He began toward his room, then stopped and said, "Oh yeah, I told Shag you'd do a test on him. He had sex with some sistah and wants to be tested."

He knew what he had done. He was hoping in the excitement of the moment to sneak his request by as being innocent. Her mood changed from fun to business. She had no problem doing a test on Shag, but she had warned both Shag and Batman to use a condom when having sex. She had made it clear to them that "when you lay down with her, you're also laying down with everyone she's been with." That Shag needed a test meant he had not followed her advice; that was his business. To expect that she would stop and do a test at his convenience when he had failed to heed her advice was hers.

She placed her hands on her hips. "And why might I ask does he need a test when I keep you both supplied with condoms."

Batman saw it coming and attempted to head it off. Today was his big day, and he didn't want to ruin it attempting to explain the irrational behavior of a very much rational man. There was only one remedy. He decided it best to sell Shag out.

"I know what you're thinking, and I've already gotten on him about it. He said he got carried away. He said he knew he had made a mistake. But right now he's worried, and I told him I'd get you to check him out. Didn't you say that if you got the Big Ninja the best thing was to find out early?"

Nedra stood and stared him down. This wasn't just about Shag. It was about black men in general and how irresponsible they could be when it came to sex. Nedra interviewed scores of people from all lifestyles who had been infected with the virus. She was able to do so because it was her job. Never the less, giving people the news was nothing less than a death sentence. She truly cared for the two of them and had absolutely no desire to see them caught by the Big Ninja.

Clearly irate, she replied, "Batman, I'm going to do this, but this is the last time. From now on, if you get caught with your pants down, you're going to have to go into the clinic or in to see your private doctor. You choose."

"You won't get any argument from me," he said, shrugging his shoulders.

CHAPTER 12

According to the directions Batman received, he was to report to 5250 Flagler Street to see Louis Rodriguez. He arrived at the building a full fifteen minutes early. Using the directory located in the bottom of the building, he determined the office was on the fourth floor. He took the elevator up then exited left to the reception area. A young black female sat at the computer typing. Seeing him, she stopped and said, "Good morning, may I help you?"

"Yes ma'am. I'm Carter Osborne. I'm here to see Mr. Rodriguez. I'm not sure, but I was told he would be expecting me."

"Please have a seat," she replied, directing him to a chair. She looked at him as if she might know him.

He could tell she was searching her memory to see if in fact she did. He did a double take and said before she could speak, "Don't I know you?"

She smiled. "I was just thinking the same thing. But I can't put my finger on it. Are you from Miami?"

"No, I moved about four years ago from Mississippi. How about you?"

"Yes, this is my home. The more I look at you, the more I know you from somewhere." She rose from her seat and stepped around the counter to where he stood. "Let me see if Louis can see you now," she said. She made a few steps down the hall then turned. "What's your name again?"

"Osborne. Carter Osborne."

He could see it was coming to her. A huge smile began to creep across her face and she asked, "Is that what people call you?"

"No, Batman is what everyone calls me," he answered proudly.

She began laughing as she retraced her steps to where he sat. "I knew I knew you. We met at Big Daddy's. You were hot on Lisa and trying to get her telephone number."

He laughed with her while she chided him about his real name.

"I normally don't give out my real name, but figured I would today. I'm supposed to start over here and wanted to get off on the right foot." He decided she was probably cool so he asked, "How's this guy?" referring to Louis.

"Oh Louis. He's cool. You're not a female and you're not white or Hispanic, so you're alright. He likes girls and usually says and does stuff that gets him in trouble. He always has a sexual harassment case going. But don't worry, he's cool to work for. He doesn't trip on power or nothing like that."

"O.K., I think I can deal with that."

Batman discreetly changed the subject back to Lisa. "Tell me, why did you let your girl treat me so bad that night. She could have given me someway to contact her. I know she said she was married. I try not to mess with married women, but she was really looking good. The way I figured, if her old man was on the job, then she wouldn't have been out."

Claire seemed more than willing to talk about Lisa. She returned to her seat so that they were closer together. "She was just tripping. As far as being married, I guess you could call it that. Her husband lies around and messes around more than he works or stays home. We keep telling her to get rid of him, but she won't. The worse he gets, the more she takes up for him. It took pulling teeth to get her out of the house. He hasn't been there for four weeks, and when he does come, it's only to get money or for the weekend."

"I'm sorry to hear that," he said, feigning sincerity. "She seemed really nice and probably deserves better. What about you? Are you married, too?"

"No I'm not married. I have a friend. And he knows that I'm not hanging around while he goes out and plays."

They both laughed. He figured her friend was probably just that. It was probably more physical than anything. He looked her over. "I hear you. I'm not mad at a brother." He checked his watch. He had arrived early to impress his new boss and didn't want to ruin it gossiping in the hall. However, he wasn't about to miss an opportunity to get in with Lisa if he could.

He stood and said, "Hey, see if you can put in a good word for me. I respect the sanctity of marriage, so I won't ask for her number. How about giving her mine, and she can call if she's interested?"

Claire handed him a pen and card on which to write his number. He did so and handed it back to her. As they turned away from each other, he saw three males, two Hispanic and one black, approaching from the direction in which he was about to head. She looked around and said, "Oh, here's Louis now. Louis, this is Mr. Osborne. He said he has an appointment with you."

Louis was Cuban but nothing like Gonzales. Batman could tell just by looking at him that he was laid back. Dressed in tan Dockers, a red Izod and ox blood loafers, he looked more American than Cuban. His hair was jet black and combed to the back. *He must have gotten his look from Miami Vice.*

Louis extended his hand and said, "Mr. Osborne, Andrea said you would be coming over." He turned and introduced Batman to his friends. "This is Tyrone" he said pointing to the brother. "And this is Alex. We all work in the same unit."

Batman shook hands with both men. Tyrone, the brother, smiled as though seeing an old friend. "It's about time we get some brothers around here," he joked. "You would think we were afraid of water it's so few of us here."

Everyone laughed good-naturedly. Tyrone and Alex proceeded toward the stairs while Louis retrieved a stack of envelopes from the receptionist. It struck Batman that she hadn't given him her name.

"Hey, you didn't tell me your name," he said.

Smiling, she replied, "I didn't tell you or you didn't remember?"

She was quite attractive, and he didn't mind saying so. Had he not committed himself to trying to get with Lisa, he most definitely would have been interested in her. He gave her a look to say as much.

"Believe me, if you had told me, I would have remembered."

"Well in that case, it's Claire."

Louis looked at both of them and smiled. "Be careful, she's dangerous."

Batman followed Louis to his office. Once there Louis directed Batman to a seat. "Andrea tells me you're looking for a new opportunity."

"That's a good way of putting it," Batman replied, impressed with his characterization. "I'm not sure if she told you everything, but things weren't working out for me at my old job. I'm hoping I can come here and get a chance to show what I can do."

Louis smiled. "I'll see what I can do to see to it that you get just that. I think you'll like it here. Just be open minded and listen to what you're told to do."

"Fair enough."

They spent another fifteen minutes discussing Batman's assignment. His official title would be heavy equipment operator. It required he complete a six-week training course on the operation of various types of heavy equipment. After which, he would be tested for licensure to operate a backhoe and trencher. Louis walked him through what he could expect from the crew he would be working with. They were currently laying a line from the airport to the Everglades. He ensured Batman they were great and that he would really learn a lot.

After meeting all the talking heads, Louis directed Batman to go to personnel to complete his orientation and sign his employment papers. Before doing so, he asked if there was anything else. Batman was content with everything that had happened and was looking forward to starting. Something inside warned him he should leave while things were good. However, before walking out, he stopped and said, "There is one thing, call me Batman."

Louis smiled, shook his hand and said, "Batman it is."

Batman stopped by Claire's desk before leaving to say goodbye. She was on the telephone talking a mile a minute. When she saw him, her voice quieted and took on a different tone. He knew what was up and smiled back.

"Tell Lisa I said hello," he said.

Claire took the phone from her ear and looked up. "Now how do you know who I'm talking to? I could be talking to my old man or my mama for all you know."

"Yes you could. But I'll bet the farm that's not who you're talking to. Now are you going to tell her I said hello or not?"

"Girl, he said hello," she said into the phone.

The person on the other end said something and Claire replied, "Tell him yourself. He's standing right here. You want me to put him on?" She took the phone from her ear and said to him, "She said hello."

He signaled for the telephone as she happily passed it to him, knowing it was about to get good.

"Lisa, this is Batman. I know you didn't think I would find you. I just want you to know that because you didn't give me your number, I had to quit my old job and take a new one here just to find you. Now will you give a brother a break or what? I have to get over to personnel, so I won't rush you right now, but I'm letting you know you'll be hearing from me."

Batman didn't say goodbye or wait for a reply. Rather, he handed the telephone to Claire and walked off. He heard Claire in the background giggling as he did so. He knew her and Lisa's conversation would really take off after he left.

CHAPTER 13

Thank God it's Friday, Nedra thought. One more day of the grind and she would have jumped off a bridge. The work had picked up drastically because of two cases of primary syphilis. A young black male had come to the clinic with a lesion on his penis. During the interview, he had named twelve contacts and eight associates. This required she dedicate her whole team to following up on the case. As a result, she had been forced to make field visits and conduct interviews to bridge the gap. Stepping outside to the DIS area, she summoned her lead worker.

"Janet, what happened to that case I interviewed last week? You know, the young woman with syphilis. Her name was Jackie. Jackie Simpson I think."

Janet walked to her desk and returned with the case. Looking disheveled, she handed it to Nedra. "Here it is. I haven't had a chance to follow up on it."

Nedra couldn't believe what she was hearing. She wanted to jump up and down and scream. How was it that she always got the losers assigned to her team? Janet had been a DIS for three years and knew the requirements. She knew the case should have been written up within twenty-four hours and follow-up done within forty-eight. She was tempted to write her up but thought what good would it do. She knew Janet hated the work but was afraid to quit. To fire her would be giving her a reward.

Nedra concealed her anger, took the case and headed back to her desk. Seated, she began posting the results. Included in the file was a blue copy of the HIV results. Nedra took one look at the results and flew out of her office.

"Janet, come in here now," she yelled angrily from her office door.

Janet heard her calling and knew she was in big trouble. She knew she hadn't done her job and frankly didn't care. There was only so much work she could do. She lingered at her desk, knowing it would vex Nedra all the more.

"Janet, Janet," came the shout again—this time more enraged.

"On my way," Janet replied contemptuously.

Nedra stood at the entrance as Janet stepped by her into the office. After closing the door, Nedra lit into her with a passion. "Janet, why didn't you check Ms Simpson's HIV results," she asked, holding the blue copy up to her face. "This lady is positive and should have been informed by now. How do you know she hasn't given this to more people while we've been sitting around here doing nothing?"

Nedra's voice had risen to a level Janet considered unprofessional and disrespectful. Janet knew her co-workers could hear and wasn't about to let them think she'd allowed herself to be talked to as if a child. She raised her voice to counter Nedra's, and replied, "Nedra, it's not my case. You interviewed her, and I thought you would follow up on it."

Nedra had heard enough. A young woman was infected and was not notified in a timely fashion. During the time they had become aware of her status and now, she could have infected a whole neighborhood. Nedra knew that Mark, the field operations manager and her immediate supervisor, would be furious. He would probably write her up and suggest she receive remedial training for failure to closely monitor her workers' activities. She wasn't about to go down alone.

Nedra decided to take official action. "Janet, get your pouch and bring it to me. I'm reassigning your work to someone else and recommending you be suspended without pay."

Janet didn't bother arguing. She could care less what Nedra thought. She worked her butt off and it went unappreciated. Not willing to debate the issue any further, she blew out of the office like a whirlwind. Nedra had taken about as much as she could. She immediately followed her into the hall. She realized everyone was standing around watching. "Don't you all have work to do?" Immediately, everyone became busy.

Nedra returned to her office with the case and slammed the door behind her. She took the blue form along with her purse and headed to the clinic. She saw another DIS and directed, "Quinn, follow me."

The young Haitian male did as directed and followed Nedra into an interviewing room. From her tone, Quinn knew that Nedra was angry. Her spat with Janet had already made it to the clinic, and she no doubt needed to reassign additional work to him.

Still frustrated, she said, "Quinn, I need for you to get on this right away. Janet dropped the ball, and this girl is positive. Take this and interview her today. I don't care what else you do. I want you to talk to her today."

Quinn thought it an honor that everyone came to him when there was a problem. In the short time that he'd been on the job, he'd garnered a reputation as being good at interviewing and investigating. He maintained a detailed record of all the additional work he was assigned and hoped that it would translate into a promotion to supervisor sometime soon. Without complaint, he took the file from Nedra and placed it in his brief. He then reached into the desk drawer, took out some referral forms, and put them in with the file. Having done so, he looked at Nedra and said, "Done."

CHAPTER 14

Batman walked outside dressed to shoot hoops only to see Brian's cruiser parked under the tree next to the Gator. He and Nedra had returned from eating around ten, and he had apparently chosen to spend the night. Just prior to reaching the Gator, a thought crossed his mind. He checked his watch to make sure he wasn't running late. He decided he had time to spare, so he ran back into the house to call Shag. If he hadn't already left for the gym, he could run through and pick him up. He hadn't talked to him since the night Nedra and he had gone to dinner. After leaving the beach, they had stopped by for Nedra to take his blood. Before doing so, she had given him a good going over, first questioning his intelligence to have sex without a condom, and then questioning his libido that he couldn't control himself. Shag had sat silently throughout, hoping he could weather the storm without Batman's help. Although Batman wanted to intervene, to do so would have turned her ire to him.

Upon reentering the house, Batman bumped into Brian coming out of the kitchen with two glasses of OJ. Topless from the waist up and wearing only a pair of navy blue boxers, he hesitated ever so slightly. "Batman. What's up?"

"It's all good."

Seemingly nervous, Brian said, "I thought you'd left. I didn't mean to take any liberties. I've been having night chills and cold sweats, so I pulled off my T-shirt. I don't seem to be able to get over this flu." He held up the two glasses for Batman to see. "Nedra suggested more vitamin C. Says it's the only thing that works."

Nedra and Batman had an open relationship. They were real friends who accepted each other for what each was. Glad Brian was in her life, Batman was intent on doing whatever he could to make him feel welcome. Smiling, he replied, "I had, but I decided to come back and see if Shag needed a ride. And as far as taking liberties, give me a break. You are welcome here. I'm glad things are working out for you and Nedra."

"Well Nedra is quite a lady." Brian took a sip from his glass.

"That she is." Batman decided he'd better get him back to her before she came looking. He smiled weakly. "Look, I'm going to give Shag a call and see if he needs a ride. I'll get up with you all in a minute."

"Sure, sure. Enjoy your run," Brian replied as he continued toward her bedroom.

Just as Brian was about to enter Nedra's bedroom, Batman remembered thinking he had seen him and cut in, "Do you have a red Jeep Cherokee?"

Brian stopped and turned to answer. "No, why do you ask?"

"Oh, I thought I saw you last week but wasn't sure. I have this thing about looking into people's cars." He was about to give him the story about it being a habit and how he'd managed to get lucky a few times but thought better. "Anyway, no big deal."

Brain looked at him as if unsure what to say or do next. Batman could see him fidgeting ever so slightly and reiterated, "Really, no big deal. It must have been someone else."

Batman didn't wait for him to reply but went into his bedroom and dialed Shag's number. *Nedra has finally gotten a man.* He knew she had practically soured on black men after her last relationship, but now Brian had come along and erased all the memories. He muttered under his breath, "I sure hope it works out, because if it doesn't, it's sure going to be hard to bounce back from." He considered for a moment how devastated she would be if Brian didn't turn out to be what she thought he was. *Lord, have mercy on his soul, how many chickens has he stole.*

Batman dismissed the thought and turned his attention back to contacting Shag. No one answered after four rings and the service picked up. "Hello, this is Shag. If you are a woman and need servicing, please leave a message and I'll call you back. If you're a man, then you decide."

The beep sounded. "Shag, it's Batman. I was just calling to see if you needed a ride." Alluding to how Nedra had scolded him, he continued, "Oh yeah, I'm sure Nedra would be happy to know that you're still pimping them hard." He laughed out loudly. "In a minute brotha."

He hung the phone up and sat on the bed. A thought entered his head of what would he do if Shag's test came back positive. He prayed in his spirit, "Lord, please don't let Shag be infected with the Big Ninja." He didn't consider himself religious. He didn't belong to anybody's church but did pray regularly. That being the case, if praying would help Shag be negative, then he was open to it. Their relationship was special to him, and the last thing he wanted for Shag, or anyone for that matter, was for the Big Ninja to take them out.

Just as he had resolved to get on to the gym, the telephone rang. He was tempted not to answer but thought it might be Shag calling back. He reasoned he probably was in the bathroom when he called and had checked the caller I.D. afterwards. He picked up, confident of his assessment. Intentionally breaking the King's English, he said, "Shag, whats bees going on my brothas?"

To his surprise, the voice on the other end was female. Light and high pitched, she spoke as if unsure of whether she'd dialed the right number. "May I speak to Carter?"

He *was* surprised now. Very few people knew his real name, and the ones who did knew it because of official business. His mind rambled to try to think of why anyone would be calling on official business. He'd sent in his late payment on the Gator and all his cards that hadn't been taken were paid up.

He decided to play along. "This is Carter. May I help you?" The person on the other end was silent. He wasn't sure just what was happening, so he repeated, "This is Carter, may I help you?"

"Oh I'm sorry. I hope I didn't catch you at a bad time."

"That depends. Who's speaking?"

"Oh, I'm sorry," repeated the voice apologetically. "I probably shouldn't have called."

Now he was really wondering who it was. Since he'd moved into the house, he'd given many females his number. It could have been someone he'd hooked up with before or someone from a club who he'd tried to. The thing was they wouldn't have known his real name. Rushed for time, he said, "Hey look, I have a game of baskets in fifteen minutes. Tell me who you are, and I'll decide if you should have called or not."

Even with prodding, the voice seemed unsure what to say next. One thing for sure, she hadn't rehearsed what she would say. "This is the last time and I'm out of here. Who is this?"

Shaky, the voice whispered, "Lisa."

Batman repeated the name in his head, searching for where he knew it from. All of a sudden, it hit him. "Lisa. Lisa—Claire's friend Lisa?" Batman could see her on the other end of the phone just as he had that night at Big Daddy's. "Lisa, why didn't you say so? You called just in the nick of time. Thinking you wouldn't call, I just finished the suicide note and was about to take my life."

He stopped long enough to hear her laugh on the other end. "Hey really, I'm glad you called. What took you so long?"

"Well, I wasn't sure if I should or not. I told you about my situation."

He didn't want to push. "I hear you. And believe it or not, I understand. Let me say this. It doesn't have to be like that. I'm glad you called, and if you like, let's just talk and see what's what. It's not like I'm looking to make someone do something that they shouldn't do."

"Oh I know. I didn't mean it like that," she said defensively.

"Yeah, but I did. I'm not looking to bust up anybody's happy home."

His mind flashed back to what Claire had said about her's being an unhappy home. However, the last thing he needed to do was move too fast. In an attempt to convince her he was appreciative of her situation, he continued, "There are too many single women out there for me to have to do that. But I would like to talk with you from time to time and see what's what. I'm not asking for anything. I'm not offering. I think you're attractive, and I would like to enjoy your conversation. I'm willing to leave it at that if you are. Now if there's anything wrong with that, then let me know and we can renegotiate now."

Lisa held the phone silently. It had been a long time since a man had made her laugh. Her current relationship was anything but. However, she was very uncomfortable talking to another man. Especially one who sparked her interest like Batman. She felt guilty about talking to him but couldn't resist the temptation of the attention he was giving her.

"Well, I don't see why we can't talk. But I'm telling you, I'm not promising anything," she said.

"Good because I'm not accepting anything. Look, why don't you use this number this evening around six? I have a game this morning and have to hit it. Maybe we can talk, and if things don't squeeze you, we can go out sometimes."

"I told you I'm not making promises, but I'll use the number again. Have a good game."

"Will do," he said and hung up the phone.

CHAPTER 15

Shag won the hustle then picked Batman and three others to play with him. Lionel and Bugaboo were Jamaican dreads, while Clay was of Haitian descent. Batman was familiar with them all from hanging around the gym. After seeing whom Shag had picked, he walked up to him and said quietly, "Why did you go and pick Bugaboo?"

Shag understood perfectly his point but smiled. "His game isn't that bad. Anyway, he asked so I picked him."

"It's not his game that bothers me. It's just that he likes drama too damn much for me. He's never come in here when he didn't get into it with somebody."

"Batman, you could say that about anybody out here. Hell, they could say that about you."

"Sure I get into it with people sometimes, but I've never seen him when he didn't argue or mess up the game. If he isn't arguing with someone on the other team, then he's arguing with his teammates. It doesn't matter with him as long as he's causing drama."

"I hear you. It's too late to drop him, so let's just play. We're alright."

"You mean we're alright as long as he's shooting the ball and taking all the shots."

Bugaboo's reputation far exceeded his game. As long as he was taking all the shots, then the world was all right. He could miss passing the ball to the open man and think nothing of it. But as soon as someone didn't pass him the ball, he'd swear he was being iced. Most often, he would curse and refuse to play defense.

Everyone who had ever played with Batman and Shag knew you had to play defense to hang. Not just any defense, but man-to-man in your face full court defense. That was their game. Anyone could

CHRIS PARKER

shoot, but defense required a state of mind. It required a mental philosophy that dictated that regardless of the score and no matter how far the offensive man was away from the basket, you were in his face. It was as simple as when the ball was tipped, you started, and after the final basket was made, you stopped. It was what made them winners. They lost like everyone else, but more often they won.

It wasn't long into the first game before Bugaboo got started with the matador defense. Batman looked at Shag to signal he may want to talk with him. What had been a nine to four lead was now a tie game. Bugaboo's man had scored the last three baskets, and if Bugaloo had made up his mind to guard him, he was keeping it a secret. Their team went up and down the court two times with Bugaboo taking the quick shot. However, after the second shot, Bugaboo failed to chase his man down court, and his man ended up getting an easy lay up.

Clay, another teammate, looked at Batman to see if he was going to challenge Bugaboo. Batman looked at Shag and shrugged his shoulders. Batman didn't mind losing and had come to accept it as a fact of life. As far as basketball, no one on the court that day was being paid. However, he did have expectations of his teammates. He believed he owed it to them to play hard and that they owed it to him to do likewise. The team they were playing was scrubs, yet that same team was on the verge of scoring the winning basket and defeating them.

Batman decided enough was enough and stopped the ball. He called everyone over. He directed his attention and comments directly at Bugaboo. "Look, dread, you have to shut your man down. He's killing you."

Without hesitation, Bugaboo exclaimed in his thick Jamaican accent, "You don't worry 'bout my man. You just pass the damn ball. If you passed the ball, we would win. I dare you blood clots tell me how to play. I play the way I want and nobody do a damn thing."

Batman turned his gaze from Bugaboo to Lionel, his Jamaican partner, and replied sternly, "Either your dread is going to play defense or we're going to loose. If he can't hold him, then let some-body else take him. But I'm not going out like no sucker."

Bugaboo was still fuming and talking with his hands. By this time, Clay had cut in and was seconding what Batman had said. Lionel raised his hands and attempted to calm Bugaboo. Explaining that it was just a ball game, he directed him back to the court.

Batman looked at Shag with disgust. "You knew not to pick him up."

Shag's look told him he agreed. Shag walked over to guard his man. "Look it's not over. We can still pull this out."

Bugaboo was still going back and forth with Batman and Clay when they walked back onto the court to finish the game. Gesturing with his hands, he said, "I do whatever I want and nobody gone do nothing. You hear?"

In the mean time, Shag passed the ball in to Clay who swung it over to Bugaboo. As soon as the ball left Clay's hands, Batman came from under the basket up the lane and set a pick on Clay's defender. Clay saw the pick coming and rolled off beautifully. It was done to perfection. Coming off the pick, Clay threw his hands up and shout-ed to Bugaboo to signal he was free for the game tying lay up. All Clay needed was the ball and they would have one more chance to win. Bugaboo looked at Clay then shot a three pointer from way beyond the arc. The long rebound ended up in the opposing teams hand and was passed down to Bugaboo's man who had run past him. Bugaboo's man laid it in for the game winning lay up.

Bugaboo saw he was beaten and made no attempt to catch his man. "Blood clot," he shouted. After seeing the winning basket go in, he turned to look at Batman and Clay before walking off the court. The two of them followed him off the court, shouting obscenities and chastising him. Lionel and Shag got between them as they went back and forth. No one really wanted to fight and everyone knew that as long as a punch wasn't thrown it would play itself out. They were venting more than anything over the fact that they had lost and how they had lost.

The second game started and everyone seemed content to let bygones be bygones. Just as they were about to walk away, Bugaboo said to Clay, "And you, you freaking Haitian, why don't you go find a dog to eat?"

Clay swung wildly as they both tumbled onto the floor. The manager ran out of the office, and along with the other men, pulled them apart. Bugaboo seemed lost. He hadn't expected the attack and hadn't prepared to defend himself. There was a small cut over his right eye and blood trickled down his face. Clay was screaming madly that no one calls him a Haitian and gets away with it. At least five men were trying to restrain him while attempting to calm him down. They finally managed to wrestle him outside.

The crowd dispersed and the second game continued. Shag and Batman retired to the bleachers as they always did when they lost.

"Man, that's crazy something fierce," Batman said, laughing. "I mean Bugaboo called him every name under the sun, talked about his mama and threatened to eat his children, and he didn't do anything. But he calls him a Haitian, and he tries to kill him."

Shag laughed along with him. Although it made no sense, Bugaboo had crossed the line when he called him a Haitian. Batman and Shag had no problem with Haitians and saw them as they did other blacks. However, it seemed that in Miami, Haitians were looked down upon and considered second-class citizens. The police regularly abused them. Only weeks before a crowd of them were beaten and arrested for protesting the abusive treatment of an insensitive landlord. To make matters worse, the INS was constantly harassing them, even those who were here legally.

Shag, attempting to make light of the situation, stood on the bleachers and announced, "Hey, that's it. The next time somebody calls me a Haitian, I'm going to my car."

Everyone laughed and some even chided, shouting out, "You Haitian."

Shag returned and changed the conversation. "Hey, Nedra got my test results yet?"

Batman stopped loosening his shoestrings and looked up. "If she does, she hasn't told me. I think it takes two weeks though." He slipped off his gym shoes. "Why, you planning on partying without a raincoat again or something? You haven't been with another freak who likes chocolate in her peanut butter, have you?"

Shag frowned as if insulted. "Who me? Not after the way you let Nedra talk to me, I haven't."

Batman knew exactly what Shag meant. Shag had hoped he would have said something to get Nedra to slow her roll.

"Look, boss," Batman said. "I was just hoping she didn't start in on me. There wasn't a thing I could do to help you. You know her as well as I do."

"I hear you. It's just that when she gets started she doesn't stop. Lord have mercy on the man who gets her. She's a nagger for sure."

"I don't know. Mr. Policeman doesn't seem to be complaining. In fact, he's started spending the night. I went back in to call you this morning and bumped into him in his pajamas. Looked like he had just rolled over and was getting OJ to refresh himself."

Shag laughed heartily. They were both happy Nedra had finally found someone. Now maybe she could give up that tough girl act. It hit Batman that he hadn't told Shag about his morning call.

"Hey, guess what," Batman said.

"O.K., what?"

"Guess who called."

"Give me a break. Who called?" Shag said, tired of the back and forth.

"That sistah I met at Big Daddy's. Lisa's her name. She called just as I was leaving." Exaggerating, he continued, "I didn't know who it was at first. But she kept saying something about she couldn't live without me. So I told her how it was and how it had to be. You know I'm a busy man, and I can't tie myself down. Especially to a married woman."

Shag feigned a punch at him. "Give me a break. I'll bet you melt-ed like snow in the Caribbean. Batman, you ain't nothing but a sucker. Next time I see you, you'll probably tell me you're about to get married."

"What do you mean I'm a sucker? I'm not the one who brings a girl home and puts chocolate in her peanut butter. No telling how many guys had been there. I'll bet you told her you loved her when you were through didn't you. You probably asked her to marry you. Come on, you can tell Batman. You know we're down like that."

Shag and he went back and forth teasing each other for another two games. In between, they talked about how things were going back home. Shag talked with his mother at least once a week, and she kept him informed of the goings on. He, in turned, briefed Batman, which allowed him to stay up on home matters.

Shag finished talking and instructed, "Hey, let me know when my test is back. And don't try no silly crap like changing the results."

"Not even if it's positive." Batman laughed.

"Not even if it's positive."

CHAPTER 16

Quinn checked his watch to see what time it was. In return for a box of condoms, he had received a tip from a local drug dealer that Jackie could be found under a particular tree during the late afternoon. Only one year on the job, he considered himself an excellent investigator. Taught by Nedra, he knew every trick in the book. It was a good thing because he needed it on this case. He had been hot on Jackie's trail for four days, and as of yet had been unsuccessful in locating her. Moreover, her case had already exceeded the time limit allowed for positive test results to be given. Compounding the problem, he had no idea how long it would take to elicit, locate and examine her sex partners. Using rough calculations, he figured it could be another week to ten days before he brought the case to complete closure. Nedra would be unhappy. However, this didn't worry Quinn. He knew he had done everything by the book. As was protocol, he had left confidential telephone messages and referrals at the location listed in her file. He quickly looked at the back of his 926 to ensure he had documented all his efforts. Satisfied, he settled in for what was to be a short wait.

Jackie walked up just as Quinn had finished logging his morning activities in his pouch. Sporting a sleeveless red top, she wore a pair of cut off daisy dukes and red high-heal shoes. Quinn stepped out of the car and approached her, calling her by name.

She heard him and looked up to see him coming closer. He looked familiar, but she couldn't remember where she had met him. "Do I know you?" she asked casually.

Quinn quieted his voice so bystanders wouldn't hear. The dealer who had given him the tip looked into his eyes then looked away. The dealer knew from the visits he had made to the health department that Quinn was from the clinic, but he didn't know the exact nature of his business with Jackie.

Quinn managed to get her attention. "My name is Quinn, and I'm from the clinic. Is there a place we can talk privately?"

Jackie played along with the game. She knew he wanted to talk, yet keep her business out of the street. "We can go to your car if you like," she answered.

Quinn turned and started for the car. Although everyone saw him, no one paid him special attention. The tree was known for the illicit activities that transpired there. Outsiders routinely dropped in to buy sex, drugs, or stolen merchandise. The rule of thumb was: see no evil, hear no evil, speak no evil.

Once in the car, Quinn started it up and drove off. He'd driven only two blocks when Jackie asked, "What do you want to talk to me about. I already talked to that lady when I was in there. I gave her the names of the people I had sex with. I don't know nothing else to tell her."

"You talked to Nedra the last time you came down. She asked me to find you and talk to you this time. Is there a place we can talk in private? We can go to your place if you want."

Jackie wondered what he wanted with her. She was expecting a date to pick her up under the tree and couldn't be late. "We don't need to go all the way there. Pull around the corner to the park, and we can talk there. I told you I don't have nothing else to say. I need to get back because my ride is coming to get me from the tree."

Quinn did as instructed. Once there he began the counseling session. "Jackie. The last time you were at the clinic, you took a test for HIV. What did Nedra tell you about that test?"

Jackie searched her memory in an attempt to recall what she had been told. "I don't remember. That's the AIDS test ain't it?"

"No it's not the AIDS test, but an HIV test."

He knew he was playing semantics. There was no test for AIDS, but for the virus that caused it. AIDS was a clinical diagnosis, and although they were instructed to say the test wasn't for AIDS, he thought it might as well have been. "Your test came back positive for HIV. Now listen carefully, this does not mean you have AIDS. It only means you're HIV positive. I need to talk with you about what you need to do to keep yourself healthy and the people you love healthy." Quinn spent the next thirty minutes counseling Jackie about life style changes that could help her body resist the virus.

All the while, Jackie sat motionless. She, like most persons having received devastating news, hadn't heard a word since he said she was positive. Quinn knew and understood, but had to document that she'd received the information. In cases like hers, he would do a re-interview a week later to allow time for the news to sink in.

"Jackie, I know the news is bad, but you have to understand what's going on. In order to protect yourself, we can't let you come back into contact with who gave you this. Whenever you have sex, you need to use a condom. That way you protect yourself, and you also protect whoever you're having sex with. I also need to give you a referral to see a physician. The physician will give you a good check-up and follow you as you deal with this."

Quinn rested a moment before transitioning to elicit sex partners. This was the part he hated most. He had just given her a death sentence, and now all that seemed important was finding who she had slept with. If he had written the book on how to conduct counseling sessions, he would have advised for the sake of sensitivity that the elicitation of sex partners come later. However, he hadn't written the book, and his superiors would review his work to ensure everyone who had been exposed to her had been notified. They would assert those persons had the same right to be tested and know their status.

"Jackie, I know this is hard news. But whoever gave you this probably didn't know they had it. That means they could give it to someone else. We have to find them and let them know so they won't continue to pass it on."

Jackie snapped out of her daze. Experiencing a variety of emotions, she didn't know how to express her shock. The part about whoever gave it to her probably didn't know made her angry. Voice wavering, she said, "I don't care who gets what. They can find out the same way I did for all I care. I got myself checked out. Let them get themselves checked out."

Quinn understood her anger. He was surprised that it hadn't flashed earlier. He calmly reasoned, "Jackie, you don't want anyone else to get this. You're mad because someone gave it to you. You have the power to stop whoever that was from giving it to anyone else. I need to know the names and location of all the people you've been with sexually in the last year. I have the ones you told Nedra about, but we need to go back some."

Tears streamed down Jackie's face. She knew Quinn was right. She was aware of the lifestyle she lived and knew the risks. Yet she never thought or even considered that she could ever be infected. Regrouping, she asked, "What are you going to tell them? Are you going to tell them I'm positive?"

Quinn's heart went out to Jackie. He had done more counseling sessions than he cared to remember. Each, in its own way, was different and more difficult than the last. He spoke as compassionately as his emotions would allow. "Sweetheart, I would never do that. Everything we talk about is confidential. If I used your name, I would lose my job. Even so, I would never do something like that anyway. I promise you, no one will ever know you gave their name."

Jackie felt his sympathy and appreciated it. For some reason she trusted word. "You promise?" she asked for assurance sake.

"Yes, I promise. Your name will never be given, so help me God. I'm not here to put your business out. All I want to do is get you and the people who might be infected some help."

CHAPTER 17

Batman drove home from work, contemplating the changes that were taking place in his life. The change in jobs had done more than a little good. Although he had only been on it a couple of weeks, his whole attitude had changed for the better. He wouldn't say he had become Mr. Responsible, but he could say he had begun to consider more than just the immediate consequences of his decisions. He had become more concerned about his long-term future and mindful of the need to apply himself in being the best he could be. For instance, his orientation consisted of on-the-job training. However, he decided to supplement it by going on the internet and pulling up information about the equipment he was being trained to operate. He spent evenings reading how to trouble shoot the various hydraulic components for problems. On two occasions, when equipment failed to function, he had been able to identify the source of the problem and make repairs. Needless to say, his new colleagues were impressed with his knowledge. They even cheered him on during one occasion that could have resulted in a significant time delay, which would have necessitated them working over the weekend.

The change in jobs not only affected how he looked at himself, but how he looked at others. At the garbage department, he had come to view the system of cronyism as reflective of the discriminatory attitude of Cubans toward others. However, the crew he worked with was composed predominantly of immigrant Cubans. Unlike the ones at the garbage department, they were very supportive of everyone, including him. His immediate supervisor had only been in the U.S. for five years and was still learning the language. From day one, the supervisor had taken an interest in seeing that Batman was taught everything he needed to know to successfully obtain his heavy equipment license. The supervisor would explain everything in the simplest details and was extremely patient when Batman was unable to correctly execute what he had been shown. At lunch, everyone ate together, talked and laughed about all sorts of things. While not ignorant enough to believe they were totally without bias, Batman could say that theirs ran no deeper than his own did.

The last change was one he could definitely get used to. It was the change in income. He had received two full paychecks inclusive of the increase in salary. The increase afforded him the first opportunity in his life to consider options beyond merely paying bills. The only occasion where he could expect a few nickels more was during income tax season. Even on that occasion, his custom was to use his return to catch up on past dues notices. However, now he gave serious thought to establishing long-term financial aspirations and following up accordingly. Over the past week, he had begun to watch financial news networks and read the business section of the paper. He had obtained a wealth of information about the county retirement system and felt ready to make some long-term financial decisions that he hoped would pay off in the distant future.

By the time he pulled off the 95 expressway onto the NW95 Street exit, his mind had moved from the job to Lisa. They had spoken just about everyday since her initial call. He was amazed at how easy she was to speak with. He was even more amazed at the range of issues included in their conversations. His normal chain of thought relegated his conversations to being more about sex, sports and drugs than anything else. On these three topics, he considered himself an expert. However, once he got past these, he found it hard to carry on a serious conversation. In the case of Lisa, the superficial rapping directed at getting her in bed had been replaced with more substantive debate on various issues in life. They had discussed their childhood and revisited some very painful occurrences from their teenage and young adult years. They talked at length about her marriage and what it was like to be a parent. They were both surprised at the analysis he offered as it related to dealing with life's ups and downs. He turned onto NE 2nd avenue and thought to himself that he was beginning to sound like he was older than twenty-seven years. She had teased him about his age, saying he was just a babe. He had responded, "It's not the years that count, it's the miles."

He changed the radio station and turned off NE 2nd avenue onto 92 street less than two blocks from the house. "Lord help me," he murmured under my breath.

He had met Lisa at local hangouts over the past weeks. However, this day, after having reminded him of her marital and parental obligations, she had given in to his insistence to meet for early evening drinks. He checked his watch as he pulled into the driveway. If he figured correctly, he had two hours to kill before meeting her at a local pub on the causeway.

The first order of business was to check his messages. He half expected her to call and cancel. She had made it clear her presence depended on finding a sitter. To his pleasure, no one had called. This meant everything was a go. He decided that even though it was Wednesday, he would use his Thursday pre-date ritual. His Thursday ritual included taking a soapy bath instead of the shower he took when he went out on Fridays. It also called for rum and coke versus reefer. The rum and coke worked slower and made him mellower. The last difference was the pre-date music. On Fridays he preferred Jamaican rap. On Thursdays he preferred contemporary jazz, his favorite being the Crusaders.

He walked to the kitchen and popped two cubes of ice into a highball glass. He took the Jamaican rum out of the overhead bin and mixed it one parts to three with coke. Content he had the right mixture, he took the rum, remaining coke, and mixed drink then returned to the bedroom. He flipped through the CD case until he found the Crusader's Soul Shadow CD. Mulling it over, he changed his mind and decided to go in another direction. He placed it back into the rack then searched until he located Michael Franks' Tiger in the Rain CD.

Yes, he thought. *This should do it.*

The last items of business were to pull out his evening attire then jump into the tub. He started the water and waited for it to come to temp. Having done so, he poured in an extra large helping of bubblegum bath soap. He laughed, thinking if he had been female, he would have gotten a yeast infection. When the water reached its high mark, he got in, held his breath then slid under the bubbles. *Just what the doctor ordered. A nice hot bath before going out to drinks with a nice hot lady.*

Batman had been in the tub for at least fifteen minutes when Nedra came in. He heard her through the bedroom door as she entered through the garage into the kitchen. From the sound, he surmised that she was looking for the alcohol to fix her a drink.

"Batman, you moved the rum?" she shouted.

"Yeah, it's in here. Come on in and talk to a brotha."

"It can wait until you're finished. I wouldn't want to disturb you taking the only bath you've probably taken this week."

Batman laughed. He knew Nedra was respecting his privacy. "Give me a break. There's nothing to see."

A short while later, Nedra tentatively walked in. She looked dead to the world. He gave her an opportunity to take in the scene and ensure it was safe.

She recognized the drink, jazz and hot bath which normally accompanied his Thursday routine. "It's not Thursday is it?"

He smiled deceptively. "No it's not Thursday, my dear."

She saw how giddy he was and said, "You sure are in a good mood. You look like the cat that ate the canary."

"Well thank you, my dear. I do feel quite well."

Nedra grabbed her head as if feigning a headache and began laughing. "Oh no, don't tell me Batman's in love. God forbid. What is the world coming to? Batman, don't tell me this Lisa whoever that's married has you strung?"

Batman sat up straight and motioned for Nedra to hand him some more bubble bath. He poured in another helping and turned the hot water to full blast. After a few seconds, he turned it off and returned to his previous position with all but his head under the bubble-filled water.

Nedra shook her head. "Don't tell me Mr. Pickem up in one night has fallen hard. I keep telling you there are some sistahs who can even change guys like you."

Resisting the temptation to respond, he smiled.

"Well?" she said, impatient with his silence.

"Well what? You said don't tell you, so I won't."

They laughed as she leaned over, reached into the bottom of the tub, grabbed a handful of water then splashed it toward his face. He slid further under the water and began kicking violently, trying to soak her. As he did, she jumped and ran out of the water's reach.

Tired, he stopped to catch his breath. She returned and took a seat on the toilet then asked, "This isn't that Lisa person is it? I thought you said she's married. I hope you're not falling for a married woman. It's enough to be in sin without falling in love with sin."

Batman sighed deeply. "Nedra, give me a break. Get a grip. We're just friends. I'm sure a sistah with it all together like you would never date a married man, but there are some married people who can have friends of the opposite sex and still know how to act."

"Me? Get a grip? Look who's talking. When did you become so mature? What happened to the one-night stands? Tell me, where did you get her from? I'll bet you five to one she came from Big Daddy's or Max's."

"Where she came from isn't important. The fact that she's married and we're having drinks in about an hour is even less important. As far as I'm concerned, I'm merely enjoying the company of a female friend. No more. No less."

"Batman, it is important. That's the problem now with black folk. We have no respect for the sanctity of marriage. If sister girl is married, then you should honor it even is she doesn't."

"So you're saying you wouldn't date a married man?"

Nedra stood and placed her hands on her hips and started to work her neck. "That's what I said, and that's what I mean. That foolishness about a piece of man is better than no man at all is just that. A piece of man won't do me."

Resolved that he wasn't about to change her mind, he settled for changing the conversation. "I hear you. What's up with you and Brian."

"Besides my legs," she said, laughing loudly.

He joined in the laughter. "O.K., besides your legs."

She calmed from her joke. "Oh it's all good. He's all but reeled in. I just have to get him into the boat. I should have that done by Friday."

"Listen to you saying you should have him reeled in by Friday." Speaking sincerely, he added, "I was serious about what I told you. Don't go thinking you can plan something like this. Women plan but men decide. The only way Brian will be reeled in is if he decides to be reeled in." Interested in her last comment and her impending strategy to lure him in, he asked, "Besides, what's happening between now and Friday?"

Nedra paid little attention to his admonition and responded jovially, "Oh I plan on surprising him. I called his job today and they said he was out sick with the flu. He's had it for some time. I keep telling him to go get it checked out. Regardless, I plan on dropping by and helping him to get well."

Batman hesitated for a moment. "But I thought you didn't know where he lived?"

"I didn't, but I do now. I checked the Bresser and the computer at Jackson Memorial. You know our computer at the health department allows us to search the hospital records. Today I took a chance and looked him up in the hospital database. Sure enough, he went into the emergency room with a sprained ankle about two years ago. I wrote the address down, and I'm going to stop by and rock his world."

The looked on Batman's face betrayed his feelings.

"What's wrong now?" Nedra asked.

He searched for the right words to use. He didn't want to offend her or infer something that wasn't true. "Nothings wrong per se," he said cautiously. "It's just that as a man, I have to tell you men in general don't like certain surprises. Most men don't like women dropping in on them unless they invite them. Besides, what do you think he's going to say when he finds out you got his address illegally? I'm not sure this is the best way to reel him in."

Slightly offended, she replied, "I beg your pardon, but for the umpteenth time, Brian isn't like most men. At least not like you or the guys you know."

"Sorry. I didn't mean anything by it. Besides, maybe I need to take my own advice."

"Which is?"

"Well there's only two ways to really get to know someone. One is to work with them, and the other is to sleep with them. I haven't done either. And since you've done one and are willing to vouch for him, I have to accept it at face value."

Softening, she said, "I agree. Anyway, it doesn't matter. Because after I show up and show out, he won't be mad about anything. I plan on going over in my bathing suit with nothing on but an overcoat. I can't wait to see his face."

Going against everything he truly felt, he said "Sure. I'll bet that does it. If he's sick when you get there, he won't be when you leave."

Nedra stood and pranced in the mirror as though modeling. She held one hand in the air and used the other to push up the back of her hair. "Sho you right."

CHAPTER 18

Batman walked into Sunday's on the Bay to find Lisa already seated. The waiter had given her a table for two on the veranda over looking the water. It was a picture perfect night for an outside date. The jet skiers were out in mass, causing a slight mist to rise up to where she was seated. He spotted her immediately and made his way toward her. To his surprise, she was dressed identical to the night when he first met her. When he made it to within a couple of feet of their table, he stopped a young male waiting a near by table. Using his best British accent and speaking loudly enough for her to hear, he asked, "My dear man, could you tell me whether that exquisitely beautiful lady over there is eating alone or with someone?"

The waiter was at first unsure of what to make of his inquiry. Stunned, he looked over at Lisa and saw her unabashedly smiling. He looked back at Batman with a smile, which he took to mean he understood what was happening. Mocking Batman's British accent, he replied, "My dear fellow, as a matter of fact, I think she isn't."

They all laughed. "Well in that case," Batman said, "would it be offensive if I introduced myself?"

"Have at it. Anything else would be uncivilized," the waiter said and continued on.

Batman made the final few steps to her table and politely reached for her hand. "It's nice to see you made it. I hope I didn't keep you waiting?"

She held his hand for a second longer than needed. "No, not long at all. I wanted to beat the traffic, so I took off a little early."

He took his seat and reclined as he did when in the company of friends. They both sat silently, measuring each other up. The past weeks had flown by with her getting to know him conversationally.

However, now it was apparent to him she had begun looking at him differently to see if there was any physical attraction.

In reality, he guessed she really was seeing him for the first time. In their previous meetings, she had gone to great lengths to communicate that she had no intention of ever truly dating him. Therefore, she hadn't even bothered to search out his detailed physical qualities. Things were different now. They were growing closer. He had gotten her to change her schedule to meet, which indicated to him this was an official date. As would most people moving in that direction, she was cataloging his physical characteristics and running them against what she liked in men. The smile on her face told him that if he hadn't passed, he was at least still in the game.

He broke the silence. "Whenever you're done undressing me, we can order."

"Me—undressing you? I was wondering if your nickname shouldn't be Superman rather than Batman the way you were looking at me with those X-ray eyes."

If there was one thing he liked not only in women but people in general, was someone who was quick on their feet. He tended to hit it off better with people who had that quality because they were less apt to become offended and more apt to discard a careless comment that might be somewhat on the fringe.

"O.K., we were undressing each other," he said, moving toward the center. "By the way, did you like what you saw?"

She looked up as if mulling whether to answer. "What do you think?"

He couldn't resist the temptation of answering. "Well if you're like most women, I would say yes."

She scratched her head and asked, "And why do most women dig you?"

"Simple, women dig me because I really don't wear underwear."

She laughed and took her napkin and threw it in his direction. "Give me a break, Mr. Casanova."

The waiter returned and took their order. At first she ordered a coke. Without asking, he over ruled her and asked the waiter to give her a Margarita. Batman went for his customary bourbon and coke. They decided to hold off on the meal while they drank their drinks and chatted. Eventually the conversation turned to Claire.

"You must be paying Claire or something," she commented. "The way she keeps sweating me to go out with you is something." Neither considered their previous meetings an "official date."

He waited a moment to consider her comments. "Well I'm glad Claire thinks I'm worth the trouble. As far as a friendly drink, I can't say I'm fond of being considered out of bounds, but I can say I'm glad you came. You've been in my head every night since that night at Big Daddy's. I was content to move on until I bumped into Claire. I don't believe in coincidences, so that means we were meant to at least talk."

Lisa adjusted her position in her chair and looked out over the water. *Lord what am I doing here?*

He interrupted her thoughts by clearing his throat. "Hey, what's up with the silent treatment? You want to let a brother in on what you're thinking?"

Lisa's facial expression and hesitation signaled she was searching for the right words. Batman knew the art of patience. Not wanting to rush her and hoping to get to the heart of the matter, he waited for her to speak. His understanding of females told him now was not the time to force the tempo. He decided, instead, to sit back in a zone defense and let her dictate the pace.

"It's nothing really," she said softly but sincerely. It's just that I think you're very nice and someone I could come to like very much. The problem is, right now I don't need any additional complications in my marriage. It's not like I don't have enough drama dealing with what he's brought to the table."

He leaned forward, closing the distance between them. "So is that what I am now? Is that what you see when you look at me? I've been a lot of things, but I don't remember ever being drama or complications."

"I'm sorry. Really. I wasn't referring to you personally, but to this."

He decided now was the time to press the issue. He switched from his regular zone to a match up zone. He placed both hands on the edge of the table and asked calmly, "What do you mean when you say this? I'm willing to give deference to your situation, but I need to know where you're coming from."

Batman hesitated to give her a chance to reply, but again she seemed lost for words. She turned and looked out over the water. He figured she must have liked him or she wouldn't have found it difficult to find the right words. He translated this to mean he had a foul to give and decided now was the time to go man.

"Alright," he said for effect. "Since you can't tell me what 'this' is for you. How about I tell you what 'this' is for me? This is I think you're attractive. This is I think you're nice. This is I enjoy your company. And this is two friends meeting to talk."

She returned her focus to him. "Talking isn't a problem."

Before she could go on, he cut in. "Look I know where you're coming from, and I respect that. I'm not asking you to do anything you'll regret later. As far as I'm concerned, this is just drinks between friends. Hell, if you like, you can pay for them."

He did enjoy Lisa's company, but the last thing he needed was someone who wasn't sure about where they were and where they were going. That was reserved for him. He sat up in his seat and said, "Look, tell me about right here and right now. Are you happy or sad?"

She looked at him as though he'd asked a trick question. It took a moment for her to realize he was waiting for her answer. "I'm happy."

"Good. That settles it. We'll deal with the here and now right here and right now, and we'll deal with the there and later whenever we get to there and later."

They spent the rest of the date talking about the past and future. He was careful to keep their conversation off the present. He figured it would only bring them back to where they had begun. During the conversation he managed to extract from her why she had worn the same outfit as the night at Big Daddy's. She had done so for him. She knew through her conversations with Claire that he thought she really was a knockout that night and wanted to make sure he found her that way for this special evening. Her sharing this with him made him feel all the more confident that the opportunity to win her over existed. She shared with him that she was even more superstitious when it came to relationships. That they'd managed to hook up and be there at that beautiful moment was significant. It took more than a second for him to stop gloating. He silently hoped that she hadn't noticed it. He didn't want her to think he was a punk or soft or something.

Nonchalantly, he replied, "Sounds good to me."

CHAPTER 19

Thoughts of her plan to surprise Brian had Nedra giddy. All day she had watched the clock. It was now 10 a.m., and to her it seemed like noon would never make it. She looked at her to-do list and began marking off those tasks she had accomplished or felt could wait until her return. First, she had advised Mark that she would not be returning after lunch. She asked that he assign another supervisor to act in her stead. That should preclude any problems about the clinic's coverage, she thought. Second, she had applied herself for one hour to reviewing cases and closing out interview records. Under this task she had placed a star to remind herself that Jackie's case was long over due. It had been in the back of her mind to follow up with Quinn on it. He had informed her that he had located Jackie and made the necessary referrals, but due to other important cases, he requested additional time in getting it written up. He assured her he would have it completed and submitted along with the case management plan by the close of business. She knew Quinn's word was good and was tempted to wait around for it. However, she thought to herself, it was already past due and another day wouldn't hurt.

The final thing on her list was to write up Janet for mishandling the case in the first place. Her desire was to suspend her for one week without pay. She had presented her case against Janet to Mark, who had in turned agreed to support the decision if personnel approved. To her dismay, personnel had rejected the suspension and would only issue a warning. According to personnel, Nedra would have to utilize progressive rather than cumulative discipline in addressing the matter. Progressive discipline dictated that the supervisor move from least punitive to higher levels of punitive discipline. Cumulative discipline allowed the supervisor to take into account the total weight of the transgression and discipline accordingly. The personnel generalist had directed Nedra to conduct a counseling session with Janet in which she advised her of pending disciplinary action if the offense happened again.

Nedra picked up the phone and dialed her secretary's extension.

"Good morning, Health Department, may I help you please?" said the voice on the other end.

"Cheryl, is Janet in the DIS area?"

"She was a second ago. I just saw her walking toward the clinic."

"Would you get her and ask her to come in?"

Nedra heard her hang up and assumed she was off to find Janet. Nedra had been a supervisor for three years, but had never gotten use to disciplining employees. She had little regard for Janet's work ethic, but harbored no desire to get her fired. She merely wanted her to be accountable for the tasks she had agreed to perform when she accepted the position. Nedra agreed that every DIS was overworked and underpaid. However, she always ended with the position that "Whatever the pay, you agreed to work for it and are bound to do the best you can."

The knock on her door brought her back to the task at hand. "Come in," she said, attempting to sound confident.

Janet stepped in and closed the door behind her.

"Come in, have a seat," she said once Janet had entered.

She ran through in her mind everything the personnel generalist had suggested she cover during the meeting. She had made notes to ensure that at a minimum she touched on each pertinent issue. All that needed doing at this time was to inform Janet of the action to be taken against her and secure her signature as documentation.

"Janet, as I informed you the last time we talk, I am taking disciplinary action for your failure to properly and appropriately carry out your responsibilities. On Friday, March 3rd, I gave you what was then an early latent syphilis case. I conducted the interview and requested that you follow up. That was not done. Subsequently, the patient's HIV results came back positive. The patient was not notified in a timely manner, which may very well have resulted in her unknowingly spreading the infection. Right now I would like to hear from you on why you failed to follow up."

Janet listened intently as Nedra spoke. She felt indifferent to what Nedra was saying. In her mind, she was anything but negligent. Nedra as well as everyone else knew the workload was such that no one could do everything assigned. She'd prioritized tasks and Jackie wasn't at the top. She knew that Jackie routinely accessed the system, and the way the system worked Jackie would receive post-test counseling at one of a number of instances. If Jackie were arrested, came back into the clinic, went for her birth control pills, went to Jackson or attempted to get any public aid, the test would pop up and someone would advise her of the results. Thus, Janet didn't see Jackie as high a priority as some of the other patients.

Janet and Nedra's supervisory/subordinate relationship had never been peachy. She had always seen Nedra as someone who craved power and who would do anything to get ahead. In the past, she had tried to reason through their differences. However, now she was all talked out and willing to accept whatever happened.

Sarcastically, Janet replied, "If you really wanted to know my side, you would have asked before you ran all over the health department running my name down. But for the record, my side is what you already know. There's more work than there are people to do it. I do what I'm able, but I cannot continue to let this place kill me."

Nedra was slightly miffed by Janet's comments. Her nature always inclined her to give the employee the benefit of the doubt. However, she wished she could fire her and get her out of her face. Sure, Nedra had told management how worthless she was. Everyone was overwhelmed by the workload, but not everyone chose not to at least try.

Attempting to remain professional, she said, "Janet, I'm not going to discuss rumors, gossip or innuendo. What I'm here to discuss is your actions or lack of action as it relates to this very specific case." She opened the file, pulled out the write up and began reading. "This letter is to document a conversation I had with you on today in which we discussed your failure to carry out your duties. Please be advised that any additional offenses in this regard may lead to more severe disciplinary action being taken against you."

After she finished, she laid the document on her desk and returned her attention to Janet. "What I need for you to do is sign and date this letter to indicate that we talked. I will provide you with a copy for your files. You have thirty days to respond in writing. If you choose not to, this will remain in your file for one year. At the end of that time, if you have not committed any similar offenses, it will be removed. Do you have any questions?"

Janet was clearly upset, but tried not to show it. Tears welled in the corner of her eyes had begun streaming down her face. She sat silently and stared at Nedra contemptuously. Nedra saw this and wanted to end the meeting all the more.

"I'm sorry if you're upset. I understand your position. I really do. But you have to understand how serious your actions were. Let's just get this done and move on. Hopefully we won't have this conversation again."

Janet leaned forward in her seat, retrieved the letter from Nedra and signed it. As she did so, she murmured under her breath just loud enough for Nedra to hear. Nedra knew better than to accept the bait, but her female, Afro-centric disposition got the better of her. She stared Janet down and said, "I beg your pardon."

Janet ignored her and pushed the letter back.

"You said something under your breath. Would you like to say it aloud so we can address it?"

Janet was at her breaking point. Becoming irate, she replied, "Yes, I most certainly will say it aloud. What I said is no weapon formed against me will prosper. You may think you're Ms. It, but your day is coming. The God I serve won't have Satan messing with his people."

Nedra couldn't believe her ears. Who was Janet to call on God when she had failed to do her job and thus endangered others' lives? Speaking curtly, she said, "I'm sorry you feel that way. This meeting is over." As supervisor, she was responsible for ensuring that profession-alism ruled the day.

She got up, walked around the desk and held the door. Janet rose and left without further incident. Nedra closed the door and took in a deep breath. She felt like plunging into her chair and closing her eyes. The meeting with Janet had drained her of her energy. How, she asked herself, did she always seem to end up with the worst employ-ees? And, good Lord, how could her silly ass bring God in on this?

Negroes ought quit it. We do everything but what we're supposed to, and then call on God.

She looked at her watch then put the letter back into the file and locked it in her desk drawer. It was now eleven-twenty. If she was going to surprise Brian, she had better get going. There was one more thing to do before she left. She needed to inform Quinn to leave the case in her mailbox and that she would review it on Monday. She grabbed a pen and paper, scribbled out a note of instructions and left it for him.

Nedra grabbed her brief and headed out the back door for her car. On the way, she exchanged smiles with co-workers. Everyone knew she had written Janet up and had begun taking sides. This was the way it was on her job. There were no secrets. If you told one per-son, you may as well announce it over the clinic intercom. Regardless, she had done what needed doing and was through with it. What lay ahead was a well-planned afternoon, which would make her forget about the entire morning.

By the time Nedra made it to Brian's neighborhood, her heart raced a mile a minute. She had stopped by her house to change into her bathing suit and overcoat and grab a few items. Just in case she and Brian decided to go out, she'd neatly folded a changed of clothes and placed them in an overnight bag. Turning onto the street where his house was located, Nedra immediately saw his cruiser. She was sure it was the correct address, but initially drove by. She wanted to get a look at the neighborhood. As an investigator, she had learned that the neighborhood told a lot about a person. The neighborhood would give some indication of his financial status. *If I am to become Mrs. Brian Waller, then I should at least have some indication of how well off he is.*

She drove to the end of the street, turned around and headed back. She had seen enough and was resolved to put her plan into action. She parked on the street directly behind his cruiser, which was parked in the driveway. In front of the cruiser was a relatively new red Jeep Cherokee. Nedra thought this must be his personal vehicle. She looked at it approvingly and for a moment envisioned herself driving it. Maybe she would personalize the license plate to read, "I got him."

She adjusted her coat hide the nudity underneath. *He may have nosey neighbors.* The day was mild for Miami, and it would not have been outside of reason for someone to be dressed as she in a light slicker. The house had black security bars on every door and window. She hoped that this wasn't a negative indication of the neighborhood. If so, then they would have to move to a neighborhood more fitting for them and the kids they would have. She dispelled the negative thought and concluded that she was getting ahead of herself, and that they could discuss all this later.

Nervously fidgeting at the door, she rang the bell. She unbuttoned her coat and held it closed with her arms. She'd decided the way to get the greatest impact would be to throw it open once he opened the door. She couldn't wait to see the look on his face. It took a few seconds for Nedra to hear footsteps making their way toward the door. She heard someone turning the deadbolt from the inside and prepared herself for what was to be the first day of the rest of her life.

Brian came to the door with nothing on but his pajama bottoms. He had been ill the last four days and was unsure when he would begin to feel like himself. The flu bug which had haunted him the last six weeks had become progressively worse to the extent he was unable to man his shift. His body was weaker than he could ever remember. The alternating chills and night sweats had come and gone but left him without energy. The persistent non-productive cough had only served to exacerbate an already bad situation. He had no idea who was at the door and was only hoping to answer it as quickly as possible so he could get back into bed. He pulled the door open and saw Nedra.

Before he could get out a word, she threw opened her coat and hollered to the top of her voice, "Surprise!"

No sooner had she said it did she open the coat wider to move closer to him. Stunned, he couldn't move or fully grasp what was happening.

In the kitchen, the real Mrs. Waller heard the shout and ran to the front to determine the source of the commotion. She made it there in time to see a naked woman wrapped around her husband.

"What the hell is this?" she asked Brain, pointing to Nedra. Her Caribbean accent became more prominent as her anger skyrocketed. "I dare you bring your whores into my house. I told you I won't have it."

Brain was dumbfounded and had yet to recover from the shock. But it was now Nedra's turn to go into shock. Catherine Waller walked up to her and shouted angrily at Brain while looking to her. "I dare this whore come parading up in here naked. This is it. You do your whoring in the street, but don't bring them here. Our family lives here."

She turned toward Nedra, drew back and slapped her across the face. The blow caught Nedra full force and threw her into the doorframe. Just as Nedra caught her balance, Catherine grabbed Nedra's hair and swung again with a closed fist. The punch landed between the bridge of Nedra's nose and left eye. The attack, along with the shock of what she had walked into, left Nedra defenseless.

"You damn whore. I dare you come to my house," Catherine screamed.

Punching, biting and scratching, the real Mrs. Waller screamed and shouted profanity as Nedra cowered to resist her. Nedra did her best to hang onto her coat. However, Catherine managed to rip it off her while continuing to attack. Nedra turned toward the wall and covered her face, hoping to avoid being scratched to pieces. As she did so, she exposed her naked flesh. Catherine, homicidally outraged, took the opportunity to bite into the back of her neck.

Brain came out of his stupor and grabbed his wife. This allowed her to turn her frustration from Nedra to him as she began whaling at his face. She landed a few harmless punches and attempted to bite his hands where they held her wrists. He, although weak and frail, subdued her. Over screams of "I dare you bring this whore in here," he attempted to calm her. She saw she could not overpower him and resorted to kicking at his groin.

"I don't know who this woman is," he said. "This must be a prank by the guys down at the station. I've never seen this woman."

Nedra heard it all but couldn't say or do a thing. She stood death-ly still at Brian's weak and ill attempt to calm his wife. Standing, the two of them wrestled in the direction of the couch.

As they did so, he shouted to Nedra, "Get out of here. Go now."

They continued to wrestle, and she continued to stand mortified. During this time, a young child came walking in from the direction of the bedroom. A girl, she couldn't have been more than four. Seeing her, Catherine ceased struggling and fell to the floor crying violently.

"I can't believe you bring this whore to my house. I can't believe your naked whore came to where me and my baby live."

The child ran to her mother and fell on her neck crying. By this time, Nedra was crying also. Not as loud as was Brian's wife, but silently as she stood by the door. Brian turned his attention from his family back to her and repeated loudly, "I said go. Get out of here now."

There was no deception in his voice. Now meant right now. Nedra knew that if she didn't leave, he would probably throw her out. She quickly picked up her coat and pulled it on. She turned weakly, stepped outside and pulled the door closed behind her. Inside, the mixture of weeping and profanity continued.

Nedra made it to her car and started it. Her first inclination was to drop her head on the steering wheel and die. *How could I be so stupid.* Overcome with anger, she wanted to go back in and tell Brian how he had hurt her. However, she knew she had to get out of there. Enough hurt had been done to enough people for one day. Drawing on her resolve, she put the car in drive and drove off.

CHAPTER 20

"Batman, put the tools on the truck. It's quitting time my friend."

Batman tipped his hat to Maurice to acknowledge he heard him over the sound of the bulldozer. Maurice in return, saluted him back and started toward the county vehicle they had driven to the work site. Maurice jumped behind the steering wheel, and Batman got in on the passenger side for the trip back to base. They arrived just as the other trucks were pulling in.

Louis was standing outside talking to a young female and asked, "How goes it guys?" He looked to Maurice. "How's Batman coming along?"

Maurice smiled. "He's a keeper. We just need to go slow and keep working with him."

While Batman was speaking to the two of them, Claire walked out. It was quitting time for the field and office staff. She was dressed regally in a red two-piece pants suit. Her short-cropped hair was in the same style as Lisa's. She saw Batman and walked over.

"Hi. I guess you're on your way to see my friend?"

In the times they had talked, the conversation was always about Lisa and her old man. In fact, he had learned more about him from Claire than from Lisa. Moreover, their perspectives on him were completely different. Lisa described him as someone still trying to find himself. Claire labeled him out and out worthless. Lisa painted a picture of her willingness to reconcile in the face of his betrayal as faithfulness to her marital commitment. Claire painted it as Lisa being ignorant of the reality of her situation.

Batman smiled. "I'm not sure. She may not want to see me tonight."

The truth was, he planned to see Lisa that evening. He appreciated Claire looking out for him and trying to help him get in. However, on this evening, he really didn't want to get in a long conversation about him and Lisa. "How about you. What do you and your old man have up for tonight?"

She laughed. "Me? I have T.V. up. And my old man, I'll have to call Mama and see what he's doing."

"What's up with that?" he asked. "Why doesn't a nice young lady like you have anyone? You're not the wicked witch of the west or nothing like that are you?"

"I must be," she said. "I don't have anybody and don't look like I will soon. The only men that notice me are married. I'm not trying to hear that though. That crap about a piece of man is better than no man at all is for the birds."

Positive he'd heard that somewhere before, he said, "I hear you." He looked at his watch. "I have to be hitting it."

They said their goodbyes then parted company. He got into the Gator and headed for 95 north. During the drive, his mind began to wander. He thought back over the day and how the work had gone. He was now in the second phase of becoming a member of the crew. He recognized three phases to becoming a full-fledged member of a work organization. The first phase was getting in. In this phase, a potential candidate undertook activities to secure a position. It most often entailed gathering information about the organization regarding educational requirements, openings, pay scale, work hours and benefits. This was sometimes the hardest part depending on whom the applicant knew. Of his own accord, he would never have been able to secure the position he was currently in without Andrea's assistance. Not only did he lack the knowledge, skills and abilities, but he was a young black male. He likened his situation to the song by Stevie Wonder called *Living for the City*. In the last stanza, Stevie said in reference to the young black male, "To find a job is like a haystack needle. Cause where he lives, they don't hire colored people." *Without Andrea's help, Steve may as well have been singing of me.*

The second phase, the one in which he was currently in, was breaking in. Breaking in referred to what happened after the person was hired. This described not only the employee but also what the organization did to help transition the employee into membership. If he knew if he'd attempted to break in on his own, he probably would have been unsuccessful. Someone in the organization usually takes the new person under their wing and teaches them the ropes. This was what he considered to be happening to himself. Maurice had assumed responsibility for making sure he knew what he needed to know to be successful. It was a sort of mentoring situation.

The final stage, one he anxiously awaited, was settling in. He was familiar with settling in from his previous job at the garbage department. At this point, he would be a full-fledged member and viewed as a contemporary. The rest of the crew would identify him as part of the organization and would hold him fully responsible for competently performing his responsibilities.

The thought of immigrant Cubans assisting in his successful development and transition in his new position did not escape him. It challenged him to analyze his perception of other races and ethnic groups. It wasn't just his perception that requiredanalysis, but his social perception. His realized that his social perceptions had caused him to make inferences. Although he knew everyone does this to some degree, his were more detrimental to establishing effective relationships with persons who didn't share his life experiences. Sure, he tried to treat people fairly, but it was in the context of making generalities. He had always felt that the reason black males got a bad rap was because non-blacks attributed their misgivings as being a result of an internal deficiency rather than an external cause.

He was conscience, based on his life experiences, to attribute certain behavior to external rather than internal causes. As a result, he was always able to excuse his own behavior, whatever it might be. He was sensitive to this method of attribution because he perceived himself to have been the victim of such biases. It was biases such as "similar to me" that had resulted in the breach of his work relationship with Gonzales at his old job. The fact that Gonzales and others like him tended to look favorable on people who acted similar to them didn't escape him. In his case this was compounded by Gonzales's selective screening in which some things done by Cubans were overlooked, while those done by himself and other blacks were selectively processed as requiring disciplinary action.

Batman pulled into the yard, not remembering the drive home.

The whole socialization scenario had completely consumed him to the extent that he had driven home on autopilot. Nedra's car was parked in the garage, and the door was up. Amused at the thought of her surprising Brian, he was anxious to get the gossip. *It must have been a wham, bam, thank you ma'am, or else she would still be over there.* Knowing Nedra, she had probably taken care of business and tucked him in. She was that kind of female—always serious, always business.

Batman stepped into the house and closed the door behind him. The house was completely quiet. He spoke just loud enough for Nedra to hear him, saying "Nedra, you home?"

Since he heard no reply, he started for her room. The door was cracked, and through it he saw a body laying half-naked on top of the covers. He immediately stopped. It hit him that Brian could have ridden back with her. That would explain her being back so early. But if he was with her, why was the door open and why wasn't she responding? Still looking through the crack, he knocked on her door. She didn't move a muscle. He took the handle and pushed gently while stepping inside.

"Nedra, are you alright?" From where he stood, he heard the quiet sobbing. He walked right up to the bed. "Nedra, what's wrong? What happened?"

Slowly, she lifted her head out of the pillow and turned over to look at him. The look on his face must have conveyed his shock because she immediately looked away.

"My Lord, what happened to you?" he asked in a calmed panic.

She made no move to respond but dropped her head back into

the pillow. His senses told him this was worse than he could have guessed. He'd known Nedra for years and knew that something terribly wrong must have happened for her to be in such a state of complete shock. He took the covers and pulled them completely over her, afterwards taking a seat and placing her head in his lap. As he did so, he held her face and examined the bruises and welts, which literally covered her from the neck up. On the back of her neck he saw where someone had viciously bitten her. The imprints had torn the skin and were covered with congealed blood.

The sight of her enraged him. He had no idea who had beaten her, but he was ready to take it up with them. Agitated, he spoke sternly, "Nedra, tell me what happened, and tell me now. Did Brian do this? Cause if he did, I'll straighten it out."

She didn't speak but shook her head no.

"If he didn't, then who did? Who did this to you?"

Nedra remained silent except for her weeping. He felt helpless and had no idea what to say or do. "Nedra, tell me what happened or I'm calling the cops right now. If someone attacked you, we need to do something." He did not intend to call the police, yet he moved for the telephone as if to fulfill his threat.

"No, please don't," Nedra said, speaking clearly between her sobs. "I'm O.K.—really I am."

Batman stopped and looked at her then moved back to the bed. "Then tell me what happened," he said, losing his composure.

She cried silently. "What happened is I made a fool of myself. How could I ever believe my dream had come true in a world where dreams never come true? What happened is I've been living in a fantasy world."

Batman was still lost. The last thing he wanted to do was make the situation worse by threatening her, however, becoming impatient, he replied, "Nedra, tell me what you're talking about. Something happened. If you don't tell me, then you'll have to tell the cops."

"What I'm talking about is Brian. He's married!" she screamed, briefly flailing her arms and fighting the covers. "I went over there to surprise him, and we both got surprised. His wife was there, and she took offense."

The surprise on Batman's face betrayed the pain he felt for her. He really felt bad about her predicament, but the thought that Brain was married knocked him off his feet. He moved to her side and sat emotionless on the bed. Neither of them said a thing, but just looked at each other. Her face was the face of a person whose only hope had been shattered.

"I guess she did this to you, huh?"

Nedra nodded yes.

"And Brian—what did he say?"

Embarrassed, Nedra turned to look away from him. "What did he say?" she snapped sarcastically. "He said he didn't know me and had never seen me. He said I was a prank by his fellow patrolmen." She paused and cringed. "He said get out and get out now."

Batman shook my head in sadness. For a brief second he felt a twinge of guilt. Surely there was something he could have done. Nedra was a woman and susceptible to female emotions, but he was a man and should have seen through Brian and the game he was playing. Maybe he was no better than Nedra. Maybe he was hoping against hope that she had finally found happiness. Regardless, he had to do or say something.

"Nedra, listen and listen good. Whatever happened is not your fault. You're probably feeling real stupid, but you shouldn't. The person who's stupid is Brian. He lied and manipulated you without conscience. You didn't know, and you trusted in someone who wasn't worthy of your trust."

Nedra squeezed his hand and lay silently. Batman got up and went into her bathroom to retrieve a warm hand towel. He returned and wiped her face from where the tears and blood had dried.

She smiled slightly and mouthed, "Thank you."

"Give me a break. That's what real friends are for." He took her by the arm and helped her sit up in bed. "Look, let's get you cleaned up. Then let's get some food in your tank."

She shook her head. "I'm not hungry. I'd rather just lie here and die if it's alright with you."

He understood she must have been feeling low. He wasn't used to her feeling sorry for herself, and he wasn't about to start either. He smiled weakly and replied sincerely, "No it's not alright with me if you lie here and die. Who's going to split the rent with me?"

Nedra smiled at him and moved along side him as he led her toward the bathroom. There she asked sorrowfully, "Batman, why do you have to be so ignorant?"

"You tell me, and then I'll tell you," he answered honestly.

CHAPTER 21

By the next Friday, things were back to normal. At least as normal as things got in the life of an average single African-American male. Things were going well on the job and Nedra was on the road to recovery from both her bruises and her betrayal by Brian. She had called in on Monday and informed her supervisor that she was ill with a virus. She and Batman had agreed that she should not return to work until her bruises healed. When not at work, he elected to hang around the house to provide her support. If there was one bright spot, it was the incident had helped them to reacquaint themselves. For the first time in a long time, they talked sincerely and openly about their relationships. This caused them to examine their futures individually and collectively. Although they had never discussed it, they knew that one day one of them would find someone and move on. Had things worked out with Brian, that day would have come sooner rather than later.

The status of Lisa and Batman's relationship was still up in the air. His sense was sometimes she wanted to be with him and sometimes she wanted to reunite with her husband. He used the term husband loosely. As Claire had informed him, her husband had all but moved out of her life. The only time she or her daughter saw him was when things were on the rocks between he and his other girlfriend. From Claire's perspective, he had never wanted to be married and had only done so because Lisa had become pregnant. Even before the baby was born, he had begun staying out and sleeping around. After the baby came, he began to do it more frequently. Regardless, that was Lisa's issue and not his. Lord knows he'd done his dirt in relationships and wasn't about to start player hating on him. But by that same token, he considered himself to be in it to win. Whatever winning was, he couldn't say.

By nine o'clock, with the exception of getting high, he had completed his Friday routine. It crossed his mind that it had been close to two weeks since he had last gotten high. He knew Dopeman was probably wondering what had become of him. Sipping on his bourbon and coke, he moved to the bed and busied himself while waiting for Lisa to call. Their last date had ended with them promising to get together on Friday. He knew she would need to get home, get a baby sitter, and get prepared, so he estimated it would be around nine or ten before she called.

Around nine-thirty the phone rung. He let it ring three times, hoping it would give the impression he was not standing guard over it. On the fourth ring, he picked up the receiver and answered, "Hello."

"Hey, how's it going?"

Before replying, he thought to himself what would be fitting for a Friday night. They had done the quiet couple thing, and he wasn't sure how much farther that would get him. For conversational purposes, he replied, "The home team can't catch a break. Besides that, everything is going fine." In the interim, he couldn't think of any thing special that was worth attending, so he decided on a straight-ahead approach. "Hey, I don't have anything up, and was just hoping to see you."

Lisa felt the same way but was careful not to seem too taken by him. She let his comment hang for a second. "We could meet somewhere if you like."

"That's good for me, but it's not like there's someplace I want to go," he answered, hoping she felt the same way and would invite him over instead. "How about you?"

"Well," she said, giving it thought. "I'm not to big on going out. I was hoping you could come up with something."

Immediately, he saw an opening. He knew it was dangerous. Lisa had made it clear that she was uncomfortable with their relationship moving too fast. He had agreed to honor her feelings but was past fed up with pretending. He enjoyed her company but that wasn't all. He found her very attractive and wanted the relationship to progress physically.

Sounding innocently confident, he replied, "I could pick up some videos and come over there."

He felt the immediate apprehension his comments elicited. He held his breath, waiting, hoping he hadn't made a mistake. If she perceived his comment as coming on too strong, she could disapprove and take her previous offer off the table. He felt stupid for having made such a rookie mistake. However, he had committed himself and couldn't go back.

"I'm not sure about that," she said. They held the phone silently for what must have been an entire minute. "I don't think it would be such a good idea," she said finally.

"What's not to be sure about?" he said brazenly. "Either you want to or you don't. If you want to see me, then tell me when and where. If not, then quit wasting your time and mine."

"I beg your pardon?" she stammered.

"Look, let's quit beating around the bush. Either you see something in me you like, or you don't. If you do, then let's move on. If you don't, then let's move on. What I don't have time for is this I'm in, I'm out crap. It's either one or the other, but not both." He paused for effect. "I know you new age professional women have touchtone dialing with all the added features. In addition, I know these new age brothers are all bout it bout it and willing to go along with it. But I'm not with that program. I don't have call holding or three-way. My phone can only carry one line at a time, so clicking over is out of the question. You're either going to talk to me or talk to him, but not to both. So it looks like you have a choice to make."

Lisa was not prepared for his response. His comments combined with his tone had left her a little insulted. She was tempted to tell him where he could go. However, she did enjoy his company and she would have liked to get to know him if her situation was different. It had been a long time since anyone had shown her the genuine attention he had, and she didn't want to pass on a potential opportunity for one that more and more seemed to have no future.

"Look, I never meant to lead you on," she said, pained by his tone. "I was honest and up front about my situation. I'm sorry if you feel like I'm using you or something."

Batman fell back into his zone. "I never said that. What I said is I enjoy your company. Now if you enjoy mine, you have a decision to make. The decision is whether you're going to take the cuffs off me or whether I'm going to have to fight a ghost with no hands. I know about ghosts and I know you can't beat them with or without hands."

Lisa knew what he was referring to. She had shared intimate details of her abandonment with him. Try as she might or say what she would, her husband was more ghost than real. It may have been better for Batman if he were real. That way she could see him for what he was. She sighed. *The thing about ghosts is people see them for what they would like them to be.*

Now was the time for him to push the envelope. Without wavering, he said, "There is no way our relationship will go forward unless we're both available. I can't fill in for someone that's missing, but I can replace someone who has moved on. If you want me to fill in for him until he comes to his senses or some crap like that, then I'm not the one. I'm not with that program. Now if you want someone to replace a bad nightmare with a good dream, then I'm willing to try. Now I say again, tell me when and where and I'll pick up some videos and come over."

Lisa switched the phone from her right to left ear. She wanted to reply but wasn't sure what she could say. She was fully aware of her real feelings for her husband and for Batman. Her hope was that she could have her cake and eat it too. She had told herself that Batman would be willing to go forward until she was sure she was ready to move on. She had no idea she would have to make a decision so early into the relationship.

She switched the phone back to her right ear. "Seven thirteen East Treasure drive. Come over the intercoastal and take a right on

Treasure Island. I stay in South Bay." She waited a second for her directions to sink in. "You better not bring a bad video or I'm not letting you in."

Batman was overwhelmed by his good fortune. If she had rejected his ultimatum, he would have slowed his roll. He already had a back up position mapped out. Fortunately, he didn't need it. He smiled. "That's a lot of pressure to put a brother under, but I think I can manage."

They said goodbye after which he went in to check on Nedra. She had spent the better part of the past two days in her room reading her bible and praying. In between, she listened to religious tapes of some of her pastor's past sermons. The one they both enjoyed and thought pertinent to her current situation was called "Sleeping with the Enemy." Her pastor had taken it from the Book of Judges, chapter 16, verses 19 through 30. His thesis was to identify exactly what happened when Samson slept with the enemy, in this case Delilah. First, he lost his strength. The parallel was that people also lose strength, and as a result, cannot withstand the opposition they are normally able to. Second, he lost his eyes. The parallel was those same people lose their eyesight. They become blind and think no one sees what they're doing. The reality is everyone sees where they're headed but them. The third thing he lost was his freedom. His desire ultimately enslaved him. Contemporarily, a desire for money, fame, companionship, or whatever, ultimately enslaves everyone. Her pastor finished by saying there was one thing he didn't lose. This thing was most important because it allowed people to recover from sleeping with the enemy. That thing was his memory. In the 28th verse, it revealed that Samson remembered God was his source, and he asked God to remember him. As a result, he was able to overcome the enemy and kill more of them than he had during his entire life.

Batman walked in to see her half-sitting in bed, watching the religious network.

"How goes it champ?" he asked.

She looked up from the seat and smiled. "Fine, how about you?"

"You know me. I'm hanging in there the best I know how. What are you watching?"

"Oh nothing." She pointed at the television. "Just another television evangelist"

Batman looked at the tube. "Oh yeah? What's he talking about?"

"Nothing in particular. He's just saying what Christians already know but don't do."

"I hear you," he replied, watching the set. "Look, I'm about to step out and just wanted to let you know. The number where I'm at is on my nightstand. If you need anything, just give me a call."

She smiled and beckoned him over with her hand. He moved to the bed where she took his hand and pulled him down besides her. She set the remote down and gave him an affectionate hug. "Batman, I'm a big girl, and I'll be alright."

"I know. You wear big girl panties and three inch heels." He winked.

"You forgot the bra."

"Trust me, I didn't. One thing though. Don't say you'll be alright but say you're already alright."

She nodded in agreement and retrieved the remote. "Get out of here." She pushed him away.

Batman got up and stood by the bed. He watched the television evangelist with her a while before leaving. As he walked out of her room, he heard her phone ring. *Good*, he thought, *probably someone from her office calling to check on her.* He knew some people on her job found her unpalatable, but according to her, they were mostly subordinate employees. Management and co-supervisors admired her dedication and commitment to doing a quality job. Hopefully, one of them was calling to ensure she was well.

CHAPTER 22

Batman arrived to see Lisa peering out of her patio window. It opened onto East Treasure Blvd, which was where he parked. After seeing her, he cut off his path to the front door and headed for the back. She recognized him and slid the patio doors open.

"Hi. I was looking out to make sure you didn't miss it," she said casually.

"Good deal, but I know the area pretty well," he replied, stepping into the bedroom. He followed her through the bedroom and back to the front of her apartment. "Nice place."

"Thanks. Excuse the mess. I didn't have time to clean like I normally do. This has been one busy week."

"Looks pretty clean to me. That must tell you how I live."

Batman handed her the bag with the two videos in it then settled on the couch. She withdrew the videos and placed them on top of the VCR. She then came and sat next to him. He gave particular attention to the placement and distance of where she sat. It was on the couch by him but not immediately next to him. His habit was to read into where females sat for any hint of how well he was progressing and whether or not he might score. Had she sat on the far end of the couch or across from him, he would have taken that to mean she was uncomfortable being in his space or having him in hers. Had she sat right next to him, it would have meant they were farther along in the relationship than he knew them to be. He accepted her sitting on the couch by him but not next to him as her willingness to get to know him better without compromising her desire to go slow.

Fine, he thought. *At least she's open minded to exploring whether we have anything in common.*

"Can I get you anything?" she asked.

"No, I'm fine. I had a bourbon and coke before I came to calm my nerves."

She laughed and asked as if unbelieving, "A bourbon and coke, to calm your nerves? What, you're afraid of me or something?"

"Of course I'm afraid of you. You're the wicked witch of the West, and if I'm not careful, you'll turn me into a toad."

In truth there was some fear; he was falling for her, and he knew it. Although he hadn't known her long, he could honestly say he was in touch with his feelings and no female had ever made me feel like he did when with her. He didn't want to come off as caught up or something. Doing so could frighten her off. Instead, he chose to do what he always did when unsure, which was to make light of the situation.

"O.K. Mr. Toad," she said. "How about a video?"

If her comment had been basketball, then it would have been a zone. It was as if she was clamping down on the middle and daring him to shoot the three pointer. He was glad just to be over, and felt comfortable with the pull up. However, he had won one battle earlier and felt he was on a roll. Therefore, passing up the jump shot, he decided to go strong to the hoop. He was glad they were together and willing to settle for a video. However, he wasn't in a video mood. He wanted to talk to her, to get to know her.

"To be honest, the last thing I want to do right now is watch a video. How about some music and conversation instead?"

Before leaving, he'd gone through his CDs and picked out his three favorite. He reached into the inside pocket of his blazer and pulled out Michael Franks' Tiger in the Rain CD. Following up his previous comment he asked, "You like Michael Franks?"

He handed her the CD, and she turned it over to look at the front cover. "I'm not sure I'm familiar with him."

"That's even better. That means I get to open your mind to new things. Michael Franks is notorious for music that stimulates thought."

She looked at him as if he were giving her a line. He shrugged his shoulders and said, "No kidding. Put it on and see."

She got up and placed the disk into the player. Almost immediately, the smooth mellow voice tones flowed from the speakers. She returned to her original spot, smiling. "Now what's this about opening my mind?"

"Just that," he replied. "I want to open your mind to different possibilities and different opportunities. That's what life is all about. It's about moving past the physical and into the spiritual."

He leaned over and adjusted his position to get closer to her then lowered his voice to blend with the music. "I've had the physical and it just didn't do what I needed done. Afterwards, I had to keep going back. What I'm looking for now is to drink from a fountain where I'm not thirsty thirty minutes later. I'm not discounting the physical aspects of a relationship, but I am saying it's more overrated than people will admit to. The problem is, too many people think the physical part is the main entrée when really it's the dessert. The spiritual part is the entrée. It's what fills you and keeps you. I can take or leave the dessert."

Lisa thought to herself that he was saying all the rights things. Still, she couldn't allow herself to be gullible when it came to the reality of her situation. Regardless of her husband having left, technically she was still married.

"I'm glad you said that," she said. "The truth is I like you a lot. But I've been down that road before, and I want to be sure the next time. I can't repeat what I've been through. I never meant to lead you on or be rude, but I have to be sure."

"No problema," he said, speaking one of the few Spanish words he knew.

He took her hand and pulled her closer to him. She didn't resist but followed his lead. He leaned back, closed his eyes and enjoyed the smell of her perfume. His heart was beating a mile a minute, but he was as calm as a peaceful sea. He could feel her eyes on him as he meditated on how sweet it was.

She leaned in even closer and said, "A penny for your thoughts."

He opened his eyes and took her hand. "One penny? I may be easy, but I'm not cheap." He leaned over and kissed her softly on the forehead then resumed his previous position.

They sat silently in each other's arms for what seemed like the entire length of the CD. However, he knew his favorite song was coming up, and he timed his response to use as an introduction to it.

"Lisa, I want you to get to know me for who I really am. The problem is I'm not sure who I am. Right now I have a million things to say, but I don't know where to start. If it's alright with you, I'd like to let Mike say what I'm feeling."

The flow of the music slowed considerably as the CD switched to the last song. He felt her relax as the music faded in and the sound of Michael Franks' rhapsody voice slowly and sumptuously fill the space between them.

"Cast upon the wind, when it shifted; I drifted. Without a star to see by, foul weather took me by surprise, I felt the sea begin to rise…"

Somewhere between the middle and the end of the song, they began to kiss. Lightly at first, then more passionately. He massaged her shoulders gently and rubbed his face against hers. What happened from there he would be afraid to testify to. If placed on the witness stand, he would have legitimately pled the fifth. The most prudent way to describe it would be to say they took flight. Once at cruising altitude, they turned on the autopilot and let nature take its course. The next recollection that he could ascertain was rolling over in bed on 713 East Treasure Drive.

CHAPTER 23

The light streaming through the patio windows caused Batman to stir from his sleep. The room where he lay was unfamiliar and alerted his fight or flight response. He popped up in bed to get his bearings.

His sudden movement awakened Lisa. "Is everything o.k.?"

Her voice brought him back to his senses. "Sure," he said, remembering where he was. "I'm sorry. I'm not used to waking up anywhere but my room."

He looked at his wrist and saw he'd removed his watch. Following his eyes, she pointed to the nightstand. "Over there," she said.

"Thanks. I'm sort of lost this morning."

Batman retrieved his watch and looked to see the time—6:30. *Good*, he thought, *I can still make it to the gym.* He sat on the bed and looked as she turned onto her back. He could feel each of them searching for something to say. The uneven feeling was in direct contrast to the night before where they conversed so openly.

He decided the burden was his to bear and said, "Hey, you mind if I cut out?" The last thing he wanted was for her to think it was a hit and run. "I usually play ball on Saturday morning," he explained. "If it's alright, I'll go play and maybe we can get together this evening."

"Sure," she said. "I have to get running myself. I left Sierra over to a friend's and promised to pick her up early. I may be tied up this evening, but we can still get together. Just let me know."

"How about I just come over around six?"

She hesitated for a second. "I'm not sure where I'll be. How about I call you when I return and let you know then? I expect to be back here by eight-thirty or nine, or I might just spend the evening with my girlfriend."

"Sounds good. Let me take a quick shower then I'll be on my way. Is there a face towel in the bathroom?"

"Sure, and the drying towels are behind the closet door."

"No problem. All I need is a face towel."

She looked at him hard, and he could tell she wanted to ask the question. He decided to beat her to the punch and said, "No I'm not just washing off. I dry off with the face towel."

They both laughed, and she rolled over while saying, "Good, because I like a man with good hygiene."

He left soon after his shower and headed back across the inter-coastal to his house in El Portal. El Portal was a middle-income, blue-collar community just south of Miami Shores and just north of the City of Miami proper. His house was actually no more than five miles from Lisa's apartment. Nedra and he had bought the house using both of their incomes to qualify. She was the primary resident. Meaning she had the option of buying him out at any time they agreed their mutual cohabitation demanded severing.

The trip home took much less time than it had taken him to come the previous night. The city had yet to awaken, and except for the early birds, no one was out. Within ten minutes, he was pulling in his front yard. What he saw caused his heart to skip a beat. A police cruiser he was sure was Brian's was parked in the front yard right outside of the garage. Quickly throwing the Gator in park, he rushed into the house.

"Nedra, Nedra," he shouted in a frenzy.

The sense of urgency in his voice must have startled her. Within seconds, she came running out of her room clothed only in an over-sized T-shirt.

"What's wrong?" she asked excitedly.

Her calmness took him by surprise and caused him to lower his voice. He pointed out the front window in the direction of Brian's police cruiser. She evidently got the message and said, "Oh that? It's just Brian. I thought something was wrong with you."

Her facial expression signaled she could see he was disappointed. She rubbed her hand over her hair to straighten it out then took his arm and pulled him into his room. "Batman, don't worry. Last night when you were leaving, he called and asked if he could come over."

Nedra's recounting of her conversation with Brian was brief and to the point. What she hadn't conveyed was that she entered the third emotional phase that follows betrayal. First came the pain, then the hurt, and now the anger. After what happened, she purposed never to see him again and at first said no.

As she slammed down the phone, the pain of betrayal had engulfed her. All of her devotion to God had gone to naught. Why was she being faithful and following God's ways if he wouldn't protect her? *Never again*, she proclaimed. From now on the only one Nedra would have faith in was Nedra. The only one Nedra would look out for was Nedra. Why should she be different from everyone else when it clearly wasn't working in her favor? She had asked herself if she wanted to be alone or if she wanted to be with a man. The latter won the day.

Batman listened as Nedra spoke without ever changing his expression. He was a man and had played the game. He knew what had and what would happen. But it wasn't for him to tell her what she already knew. When she finished, she attempted to smile to cover what they knew to be the truth. She had swum beyond the lifeguard warning and was now in shark-infested waters.

Frustrated that he didn't respond or give her an out she said, "Look, Batman, I'm a grown woman, and I can make my own decisions. I don't get in your business, and I'd expect the same from you."

Up until then he hadn't said a word. He had chosen to do all his talking with his facial expressions. However, the notion that he was attempting to get in her business irritated him. He respected the fact that she had company and chose to opt out of the conversation rather than proceed.

"I hear you," he said, reaching for his bedroom door. Down the hall, he heard her bedroom door open as Brian walked out.

"Is everything alright?" Brian asked.

Batman didn't bother to answer. Their eyes locked on each other.

Nedra spoke first, "Sure, Brian, everything's alright. Batman was just getting ready to go shoot baskets."

Brain moved his gaze from Batman to Nedra and then back to Batman. His expression changed as he realized the topic of their conversation was him. "Oh yeah, I forgot you shoot on Saturday. How's everything been going?"

For Nedra's sake, Batman felt compelled to play along. They had always promised to respect each other's choices regardless of how crazy they seemed. He was sure there had been times in the past when she disapproved of his dates.

"It's rough on rats and tough on cats."

He left Brian and Nedra standing in the hall then closed his bedroom door to change. It took less than a minute to grab some shorts and a cut off shirt to slip into. He then called Shag to see if he had left. After the third ring, he assumed he had and hung up before his answering service could pick up. A chill came over him, and he was tempted to pass on the game and just drive over to Lisa's. He picked up the phone to call her, but remembered her busy schedule. Placing the receiver on the hook, he stared into nowhere, wondering what would be the end for him and Nedra.

He grabbed his keys and headed for the gym. By the time he made it, everyone was in place. The hustle was over, and the first game had begun. Shag saw him and motioned him over to where he stood with two other guys.

"What's up with you, Batman? You've been coming late the last couple of weeks. I had to convince these brothers to hold a spot for you," he said teasingly.

"It's cloudy out, my brotha. I thought you had it going on, but there are some brothers out there who're seriously pimping them hard."

Shag laughed as he pulled up closer to him. "My test back yet?"

he whispered.

"Not that I know. But then again, Nedra hasn't been to work in a while," he answered, accounting for the delay. "I have to tell you about it. You're not going to believe what's going on."

"Batman, you just don't know. There's nothing that surprises me. In the world of pimpdom there are no surprises." He laughed as they joined their teammates.

Their game came, and they won the first easily. The other team was tired and put up little resistance. The next two games ended with them winning by close scores. Batman's team lacked a true offensive threat, but by playing their roles, they managed to win. The third game wore Batman down, so he motioned for the team captain to pick up someone to replace him. Shag saw he was through and did likewise. They moved to their customary spot in the bleachers to cool down.

Shag reached into his bag and threw Batman an extra towel. While doing so he commented, "I called you this morning, but no one answered. I wanted to see if you would come by and pick me up."

"I wasn't in. I spent the night with Lisa."

Shag smiled approvingly. "Well pimp'em hard then."

Batman kept a straight face. "It's pimping them hard that has you waiting for the results of that AIDS test. If I were you, I'd chill for a minute. It's not like that with Lisa. I really like her. We basically sat around, talked and listened to music."

Shag understood he didn't want to discuss Lisa as they did most women they picked up. "Alright brotha—I hear you. So what's up with Nedra?"

Batman felt comfortable talking to Shag about Nedra and likewise. They were home folks and supported each other when either was right but took issue when either was wrong. He shook his head slowly. "Bad news. Man, you don't even want to know. Ole boy that was supposed to be the one. Well guess what, he's the one for someone else already."

Shag laughed. "Oh no, don't tell me he's married? You mean Mr. Policemen pimping like that?"

"Shag," he said for effect. "Nedra went over to ole boy's house with nothing but an overcoat on to surprise him. Guess who was there when she gets there, and guess what that person did when she saw Nedra?"

"Man, don't tell me Nedra out there like that? I knew she's been wanting somebody, but not like that. If I had known that I would have helped a sistah out."

Batman looked at Shag and replied sarcastically, "Right. Anyway, she goes over there and ole girl beats the crap out of her. I mean she scratches and bites her and punches her in the face. Nedra looks like she got into it with Mike Tyson."

Shag doubled over in laughter.

"But that's not the bad part. Guess who I see when I get home this morning? Ole boy done worked his way in. Well not exactly. It's like she's trying to prove to herself she can be a big girl by doing what she wants. Regardless, he spent the night last night. If that isn't bad enough, I tried to talk to her, and she told me to mind my own business."

Shag sat up straight and raised his hand for Batman to stop. "Batman, listen to a brother. I know you love Nedra and all, but you have to stay out of this or the two of you are going to fall out. If I were you, I'd stand on the sidelines and just be ready when she needs you. There's no way you can make a woman see when she's being used. Only she can come to that conclusion. My daddy used to tell me. 'Son, if you hit that tailbone right, she'll go home and slap her mama.' And I don't want to hear a week from now that Nedra came home and slapped the hell outta you."

Batman nodded his agreement with Shag's assessment. They changed the conversation to talk about how the job was going and how things were back home. After fifteen minutes, Batman got up to leave.

"Hey, when will my test be back?"

"I'm not sure. It may be back, but Nedra hasn't been to work to get it. If that's the case, she'll probably get it this week."

Shag became serious. "Hey, take care of a brother. I don't want my test getting involved with all that drama that's going on."

"I hear you, Shag." Batman grabbed his bag. "I'm out of here."

Just before he turned to leave, Shag spoke up as though he had forgotten something. Batman realized it was serious when he moved closer to him to ensure no one else heard.

"Batman, when's the last time you picked up some stuff?" They called reefer everything from gungi to weed to bud.

"Oh, man, it must have been at least two or three weeks. It was the last Friday I worked at the garbage department." The worried look on Shag's face prompted Batman to inquire, "Why you ask?"

"Bad news, brother," Shag said reverently. "Dopeman is past tense. Some young brother from up in Carol City punched his time card. He's pulling the night shift for a motha."

The news that Dopeman had been shot hit Batman hard. It wasn't like they were close, but he had just seen him some weeks back and had left him in good health. Whenever somebody close to his age died, or in the case of Dopeman who was smoked, it reminded him of his own mortality.

"That's bad news," was all he could manage. "It seems like I was just with the brother. I guess that saying is true about here today and gone tomorrow. But the way brothers are falling, it's here today gone today."

Shag nodded his agreement. "Hey, I'm sorry to drop this on you, but I thought you knew. The thing that bothers me most is that I was just there no more than thirty minutes before the deal went down. I'm just thankful I was able to get out before the fireworks kicked off. I'll pass on telling you all the details since the ending don't change."

Having heard and seen enough for one day, Batman said with finality, "I'm outta here."

"Pimp'em hard," Shag offered as his goodbye.

CHAPTER 24

By the time Batman made it home, Brian had gone. Still sore at Nedra about their earlier conversation, he didn't announce himself or go to see how she was faring. Instead, he marched directly to his bedroom and to the shower. Before doing so, he flipped his stereo on and turned it full blast. He was tempted to do his soapy bath routine, but opted instead for a hot shower. He got out, took the face towel and dried off then pulling on a fresh pair of boxers. He returned to the bedroom to find Nedra lying there reading.

He really didn't want to speak to her, so he looked at her and nodded a greeting instead. She looked up, smiled and shifted her position to sit up as she reached for his hand and pulled him down next to her. "I need to talk with you," she said.

He looked at her with the face of disappointment he had given her earlier. "Then talk."

"Batman, we've been friends a long time now. I know you're upset. But you're wrong about this. After what happened last week, I told myself I never wanted to see him again. But the more I thought about it, the more I said why the hell not. Look at you. Look at Shag. Look at the whole damn world. Everyone does what they want but me. I'm the one always trying to live by a certain standard. Always concerned about doing the right thing, whatever the hell the right thing is. And look what it gets me. Screwed over. Well for once I'm doing what I want. It's not about Brian. It's about me. Some folks might say what I'm doing is wrong, and it might be. But I can tell you that I prayed about it, and God and I are fine with it."

Before Nedra could say another sentence, Batman jumped in full force. Nedra upheld a certain standard, and he couldn't see her being envious of his or Shag's lifestyle. "Are you telling me that God's fine with you sleeping with somebody else's husband?" He moved away from her in disbelief. "Come on, Nedra, you're better than that. If this is what you want, then fine. Do this to yourself, but don't do this to God. There are enough people out there saying God told them to do crazy shit without you doing the same."

Unprepared for his reply, Nedra had thought she could come in with her soft womanly way, be forthcoming and win him over. They locked glances and a change came over her. It was a change from trying to convince him to I don't give a damn what you think.

She stood and said condescendingly, "What do you mean I'm better than that? Well what about you? Aren't you dating a married woman? Are you're saying is it's all right for you but it's not for me? I'm better but you're not?"

Batman knew they had gone from shooting across the bow to full-blown war. What she said was technically right but he was sure there was a major difference. Unfortunately, he wasn't able to articulate it and it frustrated him. Rather than try, he decided to punch back.

"Nedra, there's a difference and you know it. Don't go throwing crap in my face to justify you screwing another woman's husband. Don't use God and don't use me. If you want to be a whore, then be one. Just know that the whore game is for big girls and that a whore is just one step from a trick."

Nedra stepped up to him. "To hell with you," she screamed. "How dare you call me a whore or a trick you no-good, shiftless bastard. How the hell can a muthafucka with no morals try and tell me how I should live? You worthless piece of shit."

Batman felt every word as she said them. They were like fiery darts piercing his soul. He'd been told worse, but not by someone he cared for as he did Nedra. And even that wasn't what stung. What stung was the fact that he knew she meant what she said. If she were James Brown, she would have done a three-sixty spin and shouted, "huuuh" because she spoke with passion.

Speaking angrily, he grabbed his nose. "Say what you will, but your breath stinks. You can eat shit for only so long before your breath stinks. You can cover it with mouthwash and bubblegum early on, but after a while it overpowers even that. After that, everybody's face you run into they smell it and do what I'm doing which is grab their nose."

She pushed the pedal to the metal, responding, "If anybody breath stinks, it's yours. You date a married person and it's all right. Do me a favor and remind me of when God made you judge and jury."

He was at his limit and was not prepared to go further. If he could just think of the damned difference then he would have been more than happy to tell her. But since he couldn't, he would have to improvise. Nedra and he had disagreed before, but had never gone at it like this. He moved to the door and held it open, signaling it was time for her to leave.

Disgusted and mad, she wanted to resist. Her nature had taken over and she wanted to fight. Thinking the better, she grabbed the magazine she had been reading and stormed to her room.

Before she could enter, he threw one last punch. "Pimping ain't dead. The women just scared," he said, pronouncing the scared as sced.

Exhausted, he lay down and tried to arrange his thoughts. It never ceased to amaze him how good sex could lead to so many bad outcomes. He attempted to reconcile why he was so angry with Nedra. It was her body and her life. If she wanted to play the whore role, then why should he care? She had as much right to try for an Oscar as the next sistah. No, what angered him most wasn't what she was doing, but what he was doing as well. She was as right about him as he was about her. He couldn't deny that his breath was as funky as hers and Brian's, and his judgment about his relationship with Lisa was as clouded by his emotions as hers was about Brian.

Somewhere along the way, he fell off to sleep. By the time he woke, darkness had come. He sat up in bed and looked at the clock. It was just short of nine. He had no immediate plans, so he lay back down and plotted how he would spend the remainder of the evening. He contemplated calling Lisa, but thought better of it. She had informed him that she would be back at home by eight. They had agreed that she would call him and they would go from there. Either she wasn't back or she hadn't called because he would have heard the ringer. He went to the bathroom and washed his face then returned and went to the CD case to put on his Crusaders disk. He looked through twice but couldn't locate it. He searched the room to see if he had failed to return it to its proper place. He thought back and it came to him that he had taken it, along with two other disks, with him to Lisa's and had left this morning without any of them. He picked up the phone and dialed Lisa's number. He let it ring, but no one answered. The last he remembered she had an answering service. Hanging up, he dialed again to make sure he had dialed the correct number. It still rang and rang, but no one or service answered. He hung up and thought what could be the reason.

Moved back to the bed, he flicked on the television for a diversion. During this time of year, Saturday was the best night to catch a good professional basketball game. Football season was over and basketball was the only thing worth watching. He flicked through the channels, hoping to catch the Heat or Lakers. The Miami Heat was his favorite team, while the Lakers were second. The Heat played in the Eastern conference and the Lakers in the Western, so he didn't have to choose which to support any more than twice a year. After going through most of the channels, he was able to find the Heat playing against the 76ers. The 76ers had been down for a couple of years, but were beginning to get better with Iverson leading the way.

Although Batman liked his game, he was far from being his favorite player. Outside of Iverson's basketball skills, Batman didn't harbor much respect for him as a professional or a brother. In Batman's opinion, Iverson was a brother who the black race had come to the defense of when he was thrown out of school and prosecuted for fighting in a bowling alley. In spite of what the legal court said, the court of public opinion, at least regarding black folk, had found him innocent. Many blacks from all walks of life supported him during his time of trial and tribulation. Now that he was a superstar and had found fame and fortune, he commanded the stage and needed to convey positive messages to his loyal following of young black males hoping to be like him. However, rumor had it that rather than say something positive to uplift them or challenge them to be better, he had instead chosen to cut a rap CD that was so negative that the league had to step in and threaten him with discipline if he proceeded with its release. *Go figure, we come to your rescue, and then when everything is straightened you use your influence to tell others to murder my brother and rape my sistah. Does the word ingrate mean anything?*

Batman watched the game through the second quarter while constantly checking the clock. By the time the fourth quarter came, he was looking rather than watching. He was sure Lisa had said she would call, but as of yet she hadn't. His fight with Nedra left him wanting company. The time alone afforded the opportunity for all kinds of negative thoughts about her and Brian to run through his head. He flicked off the television with about two minutes left and decided to drive over to Lisa's house. If she wasn't there, he could come back and wait. If she was there, he could say he was in the area and remembered he had forgotten his disks.

Within minutes of his decision, Batman was dressed in his best Nike warm up and riding across the Causeway to Treasure Island. He pulled around to where he had parked the night before, but was unable to find an empty parking space. Pulling out of the lot, he headed around the corner where he was able to park on the street. Rather than take the sidewalk around, he cut through the grass, which led to the front of her apartment. He saw that the lights were on and people moving about inside. He approached the front door, knocked, certain there was more than one person, hoping he wasn't intruding on her and a family member.

Directly after his knock, the door opened. He looked into the face of a very fair-skinned black male just an inch or two shorter than himself. He was dressed in blue jeans with no shirt or shoes. After ascertaining whether he recognized Batman, the man asked "May I help you?"

Batman had no idea who he was. He knew she was married, but she had not mentioned any present contact with her husband. From their conversations, it seemed as though they were growing more distant. She had also mentioned that she had two brothers and that both lived in the area. His best guess was this man was one of them, so he relaxed. "Is Lisa here?"

Batman asking for Lisa seemed to bring something out in the other male. Immediately, he knew he had guessed wrong. Henry, her husband, released the handle and stood tall as if trying to appear larger. Batman could definitely feel him taking a second look at him, sizing him up. His voice changed to reflect a slight edge. "Sure. Who should I say is calling?"

Batman had been in the game a long time and didn't need glasses to see what he had walked into. He hadn't come looking for a battle, but after the day he had lived through, he could honestly say if one came then one came. He thought about General Patton's response when asked the key to being successful in battle, "Get there first and have the most men." Batman felt he was behind the eight ball because her husband had gotten there before him, and Batman was alone and didn't know if her husband had someone with him. Regardless, he was feeling slightly reckless and decided the best way was to play it heads up.

Batman changed his tone to exude confidence that matched the edge in her husband's voice. "Tell her it's Batman. I forgot my CD's when I left this morning."

As intended, his statement caught his adversary in the kidneys, and he flinched. Batman had learned through the school of hard knocks that if you drop a quarter and someone flinches, then you could get him with a fifty-cent piece.

Henry hesitated. He wanted to speak but stepped away from the door and went back into the bedroom. Prior to doing so, he pushed the door up without closing it. Batman wasn't about to let him recover from his earlier remark. Henry had failed to invite Batman in, leaving him standing outside without the least bit of courtesy. Batman took the opportunity to invite himself in. He headed for the couch to take a seat but thought better of it. He didn't want her husband to catch him seated. Allowing him to stand over Batman might have given Henry false confidence that could have lead to the man making a bad decision.

Batman heard him in the back talking harshly to Lisa.

"There's a guy at the front door who said he left his CDs here. What's this all about?"

"Say what?" she replied nervously. "I don't know?"

"Then maybe you need to go speak with him since he seems to know," he responded bitterly. "He said he left his CDs like he's a regular. Don't tell me somebody has been pushing up on my house? I know good and damn well you haven't brought anybody up in here around my daughter."

Sounding panicked, she replied, "I don't know what you're talking about. Haven't nobody been up in here but Sierra and me."

"That's what you say. The guy out there says different. All I'm saying is you've been crying about us working out our differences, and now I have to be disrespected like this? I don't think so. I don't need a man walking up on me in my house while I'm here with my family. Maybe I should leave?"

"No. Please." Lisa's cry carried from the bedroom. "Henry, don't go. Please, you just got here. This must be a mistake."

"That's what you say," he replied, playing his hand to the hilt. "You need to get this straightened out before I leave. I didn't come home to be disrespected. This is why I haven't been home. I don't need anybody disrespecting me in my own house."

It was clear to Batman that ole boy could care less about him being there. Batman was hardly the issue at all. Henry was talking about being disrespected in his own house when according to what Lisa and Claire had told Batman previously, he never paid a penny toward the rent. Regardless, that was none of his business, but if

Henry had been angry, he would have been more accusatory. No, what he wanted was to use Batman's presence to justify leaving and going back to his girlfriend.

Batman heard movement and knew they were on their way back in. By this time, he had moved to the stereo to get the three disks. Lisa walked in first with Henry close behind. She came to a stop, and he slid around and behind her so he could get a good look at Batman and Lisa in the same view.

"Oh, Batman, it's you," she said.

The nervousness in her voice was evident. She turned as though searching for a good excuse for why Batman was there. The look on Henry's face turned stone cold.

"Henry, this is Batman. He works with Claire at the water department. I borrowed three of his CDs, and he just came for them." She turned from her husband to Batman. "Batman, your disks aren't here. I dropped them off at Claire's house this afternoon. She said she would give them to you Monday."

"That's cool," Batman said, flashing a million-dollar smile at ole boy. "I'll get them from her whenever."

Tempted as Batman was to blow her cover, he remained calm. He decided his game plan was only going as far as needed to let Henry know he wasn't dealing with a punk; it was a man thing. Nothing could be gained from hurting Lisa or whatever hopes she had of reconciling her marriage. As far as he was concerned, all was fair in love and war.

Batman turned from smiling at Henry and looked at her. He knew he should be leaving. However, the longer he stood the more agitated he became. Like a fool, he had broken the same rules he had preached to Nedra about. *Never drop in unannounced,* he had counseled. *Never surprise your significant other.* "I guess I'll be going." He turned to leave, but the pot that had been simmering was now boiling over. He turned back to the two of them. "Just one thing. When did I go from being drama and complications to being a mistake?" he asked, referring to her comments to Henry.

Stunned, she replied, "I beg your pardon?"

"When did I become a mistake? I heard you tell Henry there must be some mistake. Is that what I am now?" he asked, flashing all thirty-two.

Lisa, totally lost for words, looked pleadingly at him as she searched for what to do. It was as though she was begging him to go along and act as if nothing had happened. He, in return, just stared at her. They had agreed to make no promises, but he never expected to be out and out lied to. Batman realized that she knew when he had left that morning that Henry would be there that evening. He couldn't prove it and didn't need to, but the look on her face screamed guilty as charged. They stood and stared for a full minute without saying a word. Everyone was waiting for someone else to speak.

"She said Claire had them and you would get them Monday," Henry interjected, speaking more politely than he had during Batman's entire stay. He stepped to the door and held the handle. "Is there anything else?"

Batman continued to stare at Lisa. Strangely, he felt betrayed but not as angry with her as at himself. The temptation to make a scene gnawed at his insides. The nigga in his right pocket was itching to get out. There was no doubt in his mind that ole boy couldn't do anything with him. As much as he wanted to act ignorant, there was nothing that causing drama would accomplish. Her husband wouldn't relinquish his hold on her until he decided to.

Batman replied collectedly, "No—there's nothing else." He was prepared to walk past Henry and out the door without saying goodbye dog, goodbye cat or anything. Instead, he pulled abreast of him, looked him in his eyes and said loud enough for her to hear, "Pimp her hard homeboy."

He made a beeline for the Gator and got out of there. He was in a sure enough foul mood. He didn't want to go home, but didn't want to go out either. He had really been looking forward to spending some time with Lisa, but now that was a thing of the past. He had been out there long enough to realize what type she was. If he was willing to do to her what ole boy was doing, then they could have done business. However, it wasn't in him to use or abuse, at least not to that extent, so he resolved that their fleeting relationship was just that.

A thought crossed his mind to head over to Shag's. Still early for Shag, he was probably lounging at home. Batman dismissed the idea, thinking he'd had his full of him also. He was all dressed up with no place to go, so he decided to do like the guys on *Cheers* and go to a place where everybody knew his name. For better or worse, that place was home.

Batman arrived back, went straight into his bedroom and fell onto the mattress. He had no desire to watch television or to talk with Nedra. Reading a book was out of the question. That left him with nothing to do but think, and he was in no mood to do that. It hit him that he hadn't gotten up with any of his old girls in a while.

He went to his dresser and rummaged through the top drawer for someone to call. He went over the pros and cons of each then decided on Rene. He took the piece of paper she had written her number on and read over it silently. He repeated her number as he dialed.

Her phone rang four times before a male voice picked up. After the drama with Lisa and her old man, his first thought was to hang up. He held the phone while the male voice asked for the second time, "Who's speaking?"

Batman decided what the hell. "May I speak to Rene."

The voice hesitated for a second as if unsure what to say. "Who should I say is calling?"

"Tell her it's Batman." Just in case that wasn't enough to get her to the telephone, he added, "I met her at Big Daddy's and she told me to call her."

His last addition must have satisfied the speaker, because he heard him holler, "Mama, somebody named Batman wants to speak with you."

In the background he heard her holler back, "Who?"

The male voice responded, "Batman. He said he met you at Big

Daddy's."

Batman waited patiently for Rene to come to the telephone. He used the time to calculate her age. The male who had answered sounded at least eighteen or twenty years old. He'd guessed her age to be thirty, tops. *Boy was I wrong.*

Rene picked up the telephone. "Hello. Who's speaking?"

"Rene, it's Batman. You remember we met at Big Daddy's and you stayed with me one night."

"You know—you spent the night." He hoped she would remember him without him bringing up he had made her catch the bus.

Consistent with how the day had gone, she replied, "Oh yeah, I remember. You refused to let me shower. You refused to take me home. And, you got that girlfriend who thinks she's all that."

"Nooooooo. No, no, no. You got it all wrong. It's not like that at all. First, Nedra is my roommate and not my girlfriend. I don't like women like her. I like ladies like you. You know, someone who's fine as wine and right to dine. Second, why are you getting down on a brother? I let you in on what the deal was. I didn't let you shower or take you home because of my work situation. I wanted to spend some time, but I had to get to work."

He depended on his line about her not being like Nedra and being fine to win the day. He felt a change in her tone as she replied, "Well still that ain't no reason to act like you did. I don't like people rushing me."

"That's cool," he said, giving in to her ire. "I can handle that. I'm not rushing you now. And tomorrow isn't a workday. So what's your excuse for getting down on a brother now?"

"I'm not getting down on you. I'm just letting you know what happened."

"Look, what do you have up for tonight? I was hoping I would get a chance to make it up to you."

"What do you have in mind?"

Under normal circumstances, he wouldn't have even offered to take her out. However, he was hard pressed and knew that he had to put something on the table or else it was a no go. The problem—he didn't want to lay down any heavy bucks on someone he could have gotten on the cheap. If only he had known what was on the table, he could have come in just over that. That would have been a win, win deal. She would have won by getting a better offer, and he would have won by not having to spend much more than the next man.

He'd noticed women failed to understand how talking about their past relationships affected potentially new ones. They met a man, and the first thing they'd do was start talking about their old man and how he did or didn't do this or that. He figured they did it as a compliment to inform the brother they appreciate him over their past suitor. What they failed to realize was how a brother used this information. The way he saw it, men compared themselves by what they had to do or pay to get in as compared to what the other guy had to do or pay. He'd surmised that the male mentality was such that regardless of how much he liked the product, if he overpaid, his ego wouldn't let him enjoy it.

An analogy of going to the same dealership to buy a new Mercedes Benz came to his mind. Both guys buy the exact same type of car. Both guys have dreamed of owning a Benz their entire lives. They go home and both guys are happy. However, the next day one guy comes into information that the other got his car for ten thousand less. His first reaction is to return the car. He will not rest until he either takes the car back, or negotiates a lower price. He saw it the same way with women. Once a guy realized that he's paid more than the last guy for the same product, he will either give it back or negotiate a lower price. More often than not, he negotiated a lower price by cutting down on meals out and gifts.

How many sistahs complain about brothers not treating them as they did when they first hooked up? They criticize the brother when they should be criticizing themselves. He shook his head, thinking they were the ones who shot off their mouths and advertised the going price.

"Well how about we go to Mickey D's or something?" Batman asked.

"Thanks," she said dryly, alerting Batman he'd come up short, "but I told an old friend that I'd go to the movies with him. He's probably on his way, and I don't want to do him bad. How about giving a call some other time?"

Batman interpreted what she said as he'd offered a combo meal and the other guy offered a combo with a movie. He didn't blame her for taking the better deal. At least she'd been tactful enough, considering he'd called at the last minute. Disappointed, he replied, "Will do."

CHAPTER 25

Nedra returned to work Tuesday morning full of energy and new resolve. Her bruises and scratches had all but healed. She used extra rouge to cover the marks that still showed. Sitting at her desk, she reflected on what had happened over the last week. She was still uneasy about the situation with Brian, but had come to accept that it was what it was. She had no desire to keep him on a long-term basis but would do to him what he had done to her. She would use his company until she decided to move on. She did have some angst about messing with a married man, and one with a small child at that but told herself so what. If she didn't think about herself, then no one else would.

From her desk, she started through the pile of materials that had stacked up in her box. As she did every morning, she compiled a to-do list in which she prioritized the tasks according to their level of importance. She focused her mind on accomplishing everything on the list and felt confident that if she received four uninterrupted hours, she could do so.

The first thing on her list was to close out the case on Jackie Simpson. Quinn, as directed, had written up the case and left it in her box. It had sat untouched for the entire time she was absent. She was tempted to close it as an unable to locate case and reopen it later. However, Quinn had managed to elicit the names of new sex partners. This required her to review and approve the case management plan.

Nedra opened the case and read the write up. It was straightforward and based on her original interview. She looked over her notes regarding the sex partners and saw that Quinn had attempted to contact everyone initially named to her. She signed her initials to each form 2936 and placed them in a different stack for filling in the record room. The next thing was to check to make sure that Jackie's HIV results had been posted to the medical record and that her contacts were counseled and tested for both syphilis and HIV infections. She found the location where the test results were on the record and identified that this too was complete. Her mind flashed back to the day she had done the interview and given it to Janet. Had Janet done anything, the case could have been closed within one week. Now, it was likely to be flagged by Mark and included as fodder in her evaluation. Nedra thought to herself, regretfully, that she should have given it to Quinn to start with.

The last thing to do was for her to verify the additional sex partners Quinn had elicited. He had told her informally that Jackie had been reluctant to open up for fear of her safety. After much convincing that everything they said confidential, she had given additional names. She moved down the list, and surmised that Jackie had named four more partners. Three were provided with nicknames and beeper numbers, but no addresses where they could be located. Jackie was only able to provide the location where they sold drugs. The fourth partner was named Brian Unk. Unk was the code used to identify unknown. Brian Unk and Jackie had had sex on at least four occasions over a three-week period. The write up said she had not named him because it had been close to a year since they last had sex. Quinn, being meticulous, had decided to take the information anyway and let Nedra decide whether Brian should be followed up or not. No information was provided as to Brian Unk's home address or telephone number. Included were his approximate age, height, complexion and distinct features. Nedra read the information carefully and couldn't help but think that her Brian had the same identifiers. What she saw next knocked her flat. Under additional locating information, Quinn had written, *works for Miami police department. Patrols Overtown area. Car number 5612.*

Nedra couldn't believe what she had read. Hyperventilating, she was so unsure of her eyes that she read it again. Sure enough, Jackie was alleging to have had sex with her Brian. Her mind raced back over the last six weeks. He had constantly complained of body aches, flu like symptoms, and night chills—classic symptoms of the virus. Nedra wanted to run out of the building but couldn't. Her legs would not support her weight. She leaned her head on the desk and began to cry. She couldn't believe that Brian had exposed her to the virus. There had to be some mistake. Brian would never have sex with a girl like Jackie. During the time they had been seeing each other, he had said as much himself. He had told her he was looking for someone professional, intelligent and progressive to spend his life with and that he didn't have time for someone only wanting to have sex. She was the type woman Brian would invest his efforts in securing, not Jackie. Over and over Nedra read the file, hoping she had made some mistake, but over and over she realized that Jackie had indeed named Brian.

A knock at her door caused her to stop crying and look up. She sat still, hoping the person would go away. Her whole body was numb, and she couldn't speak had she wanted to. Slowly, the door came open. Mark, her supervisor, peered around the edge. He saw her sitting there like a zombie and ran in.

"Nedra, what's wrong with you? Are you alright?" he asked, voice laced with worry. Nedra didn't answer but sat completely still. Mark reached for her right wrist and placed his fingers over it as though searching for a pulse. "If you're not feeling well you can go. I know you wanted to come back and get some work out, but we don't need you if you're not well."

Nedra nodded her head. "Yes, that's it," she said barely audible.

"Look, let me get your things and help you to your car," he said, lifting her by the arm. "Do you think you can make it home safe?"

Again, Nedra nodded. With Mark's assistance, she stood and grabbed her purse. Summoning her strength, she went out the back door and into the parking lot. She made it home to an empty house. She had no idea what to do or where to turn. Batman had warned her of the possible outcome of continuing a relationship with Brian. Under normal circumstances, she would have called him. However, her unwillingness to heed his advice led her to believe he had washed his hands of the whole affair. All of a sudden, a thought crossed her mind. What if Jackie were lying or if she was simply mistaken? Sure, it had to be a mistake. She had just found out she was positive and was assigning blame to any and everyone she knew. What if Brian had picked her up for something and now she decided she could get even?

Nedra knew that with HIV, the first emotion was denial and the second, anger. Quinn's write up described Jackie not hearing anything after first receiving the news. He later described her as being angry and saying she didn't care if anyone else was infected. Grasping for straws, all she could consider was that must be it. *That must be why Jackie named her Brian. She was angry and directing her ire at him.*

Nedra felt an instant rush of relief. Surely, she was right. She dropped her purse on the couch and ran into her bedroom, picked up the telephone and dialed Brian on his beeper. After the tone, she put in her number and then inputted *-911. She held the phone long enough to hear the messenger thank her and then hung up. Within minutes her phone rung. It was Brian on the other end.

"Nedra, what's wrong? Why did you use the emergency code?"

Nedra was unsure of just how to break the news to Brian. She didn't know up from down. Things were moving so fast everything was a blur. As best she could, she tried to control her emotions.

"I'm not feeling well. Could you please come over?"

She could see Brian's face in her mind. She was sure he would be upset over her beeping him and then using the emergency code simply because she did not feel well. It was only his second day back, and he was running behind on his paperwork. He and Nedra had just spoken that morning and agreed that each of them needed to get back into the flow of work. Now here it was no less than three hours later, and she was already calling.

Brian thought that the current relationship with Nedra was worth saving. It was a low maintenance, no commitment agreement. He had no desire of leaving his wife for her and after what had happened Nedra had no desire for him to be her long-term partner. All the same, he could just as well do without the headache. He knew that sooner or later she would cut him loose, but he didn't want to do anything to speed up that day.

He attempted to cover his frustration, saying, "Can it wait until shift change?"

Nedra was too far in to pull back. She didn't want to compromise her plan of action. She needed to talk to someone before she went out of her mind. Sounding insistent, she replied, "No. I need to see you, and I need to see you right away."

Brain held the phone without speaking. *This is what I get for messing with high-minded black females. They think because they have a couple of degrees and work for the man that a brother really should want to hear what they have to say. The bottom line is, a real brother is going to be in charge whether they have more degrees than a thermometer or have none at all.*

Nedra interrupted his thoughts. "Did you hear me? I need to see you right away."

Brian calculated he had a twenty-minute window that would allow him to stop by without anyone knowing he wasn't on duty. Sighing, he said, "O.K., but I can't stay long. They've been cracking down lately, and I don't need any trouble. I'll be there in ten to fifteen minutes."

Nedra sat looking out of the window the entire time. She saw Brian pull up and jump out of the car. Almost at a run, he came to the door and rang the bell. She opened the door and practically pulled him into the house.

"What's wrong, Nedra," he asked sharply, wanting to know what lay behind her bizarre behavior. "What's happened with you?"

Her plan to remain composed jumped out the window. Thoughts swirling in her head of having possibly been exposed to someone HIV positive had left her petrified. "Oh, Brian," she cried, "there's been a terrible mistake."

Brain led her to the couch where they sat down then took her hand in his. "Nedra, what are you talking about? I have no idea what you're saying."

Nedra had no resistance left. Her intent was to tell him without seeming weak or petty. Before she knew it, she'd blurted out, "Brian, a girl came into the clinic with AIDS. One of my workers talked to her. She said she had sex with you."

Brian's whole expression and attitude changed. His defensive mechanisms kicked in and he exclaimed loudly, "She said what?"

He started to speak but caught his breath before stating, "I know didn't nobody come in and say nothing about me. Who said this? This is nothing but a lie, and I won't have anyone lying on me saying I got AIDS."

He took Nedra by her shoulders and held her firmly, insisting sternly, "Tell me who said this. I'll take care of it. I'm not in the mood for screwing around with folks and their lies."

Frightened by Brian's behavior, she attempted to sound composed. "Look, it's not important. I knew it was just a mistake. I just needed to talk with you and hear it from you."

Brian heard yet didn't hear her. All that was on his mind was that someone had gone in and given his name. He wasn't about to be pacified into not confronting them. Releasing Nedra, he looked into her eyes and spoke calmly, but resolutely. "Nedra, I really need to know who it was. Just tell me who said this. I know we'll never have a long-term relationship, but I thought whatever happened we would always be friends. Now I'm asking you as a friend. I want to know who told you this, and I don't want you to lie to me."

Nedra, terrified by the wildness in his eyes, remained silent. As his grip on her tightened, she prayed for Batman or anyone to show up.

"Give me the name, Nedra," he bit out, shaking her.

Her head told her to lie. His tight hold on her told her he'd harm her if he suspected she lied. Emotionally pinned in a corner, she whispered, "Jackie Q, we don't have her last name." Tears streamed down her cheeks. "She came into the clinic with syphilis and came back positive for HIV."

Brian searched his memory trying to associate the name with a face. Try as he might, he came up empty. His conscience told him that this didn't mean a thing. There were tons of women he had had sex with and didn't know their names. He picked them up on petty crimes and suggested sex as a means for him not charging them. Most were more than willing to do anything to oblige him rather than go to jail.

Speaking slowly, he directed his inquiry to Nedra. "Nedra please think. What did she look like, and where did she say she knew me from?"

Nedra was glad Brian had calmed down. It gave her time to regain some composure. She knew she had told him too much and didn't want to reveal any more. Feeling a need to protect Jackie, she decided to give him generic rather than specific information. The name Jackie was common; hopefully, he'd never place her. "I don't remember her exactly, except that she's slim and from around the Liberty City area."

Brain knew Nedra was being intentionally unhelpful. He could push more, but he was at the wall. He picked his mind and concluded he knew who his accuser was. He remembered having picked up a girl from that area named Jackie at least four or five times. His impression was that she walked around in daisy dukes attempting to appear hot. His picking her up and offering her an opportunity to have sex rather than go to jail was merely him giving her a chance to do what she really wanted to do, which was be a whore. He surmised that if she didn't want to be one, then she wouldn't dress the way she did and do the things he knew she was doing.

Satisfied, Brain remained calm, took Nedra's hand and squeezed it lightly to say thank you. A thought ran through his head, and he acted on it. He leaned over, kissed her forehead and then her neck. He whispered in her ear he loved her and wanted to live the rest of his life with her. He attempted to slide a hand under her blouse.

She grabbed his wrist. "No. I need to be alone right now and think you'd better go."

CHAPTER 26

Exactly one week later, Nedra woke up late. She arrived in the office around eleven o'clock and headed for the clinic. On her way there, she passed her co-workers and subordinates. They greeted her with strange looks on their faces. As she entered the clinic, she passed Quinn.

"Good morning," she greeted him jubilantly.

Quinn, in turn, did not stop to acknowledge her but stepped past her as he continued to walk silently toward the Hadley building. She followed him with her eyes. *What's his problem?* She had never seen him like that. *He must be having a bad day.* She continued on, walking to the check-in window and offering a cheery "good morning" to the clerks.

Everyone mumbled "good morning" in return. However, it seemed as though their hearts were not in it. It struck her that everyone was acting funny. She thought to herself, maybe something had happened in the clinic that she was unaware of. She had been absent the better part of the last week and anything could have happened to put everyone in a somber mood. As she turned to head down the hall, she was stopped by a voice calling her name. Turning, she saw it was Mark.

He approached to within arm's length and said brazenly, "Nedra, get your things and meet me in my office. There're some things we need to discuss."

Mark's tone and enraged eyes worried Nedra. She couldn't think of any reason why he would need to see her. She had been out for about a week, but she had provided an appropriate excuse. "Is everything alright? I was just about to check on the clinic staff to make sure we're ready for the rush."

Impatient, he said sternly, "Do as I say, and just meet me there with your things."

Bewildered, she headed out of the clinic and upstairs to his office where she found Quinn seated alongside two persons. She immediately recognized them to be from personnel, previously assigned to cover health department matters. She had met them while dealing with Janet's disciplinary action.

Mark walked in behind her and directed her to take a seat then walked around to his desk and took a seat in his chair. He looked at everyone uneasily and said to her, "Nedra we have a serious problem. As a supervisor, you know that there is nothing more important in this job than confidentiality. If confidentiality is broken, someone could be hurt very bad or even killed. It's the first thing we teach, and it's one of the few things that can get you fired on the spot."

He stopped and looked at Quinn. "Quinn here tells us that he provided you with a case in which a young lady named an officer named Brian. He claims you read the case and told Brian who named him. As a result, this officer went and located the young lady and pistol whipped her. As we speak, she's laying over at Jackson Hospital in extremely serious condition." Mark gave his comments time to sink in.

Nedra was at a loss for what to say or do. She wanted and needed to say something, but couldn't. Quinn sat looking at her silently, with tears in his eyes, able to conceal his anger toward her.

Speaking contemptuously, Quinn broke into the conversation. "I can't believe after all the stuff you taught us that you'd go and do something like this. It was you who always said we were here for the patients." He stopped long enough to wipe his face. "I really believed in you. That's why it never bothered me that you supervised by the book. Now look at you. You wrote Janet up for not doing her work, but what about you? At least Janet didn't almost get somebody killed."

Quinn's last statement about almost getting Jackie killed struck like a lightening bolt. Everyone knew the significance of confidentiality, especially Nedra. As the day's had passed, Nedra had convinced herself that she'd over reacted with Brian. He wasn't the monster she'd given Jackie's name to. But now this. She hated herself for allowing fear and anger to rule her. She closed her eyes and did something she hadn't done in a while, prayed for forgiveness.

The two other persons merely looked as though indifferent. They had worked with Nedra on disciplining Janet. Their opinion of her was very high, but that was then and this was now. They had no more desire to see her punished as they had Janet. In Janet's case, they were able to argue moderation. However, in the case of breach of confidentiality, everyone knew the rule—termination without appeal.

Having received no indication Nedra would speak, Mark went on. "Right now we have turned this over to internal affairs. They will be interviewing the young woman and the officer. I notified the police chief and the district administrator for the health department. In addition, I called in personnel to assist with how to deal with this. I want you to know you have the right not to say anything. In fact, in light of the charges against you, I would advise that you didn't speak. However, as of right now you are suspended without pay. If after having concluded the investigation, we find you in fact you breached confidentiality, you will be summarily fired. In addition, we will seek criminal charges against you. I hope you understand we have no choice in this matter. The ability to keep patient's health information confidential is an absolute must if we are to do our jobs."

Nedra sat without saying a word. She had heard everything Mark said. However, the roller coaster ride of the past week had left her numb to anything. If what she heard was correct, she was being fired and could go to prison. She rose, stepped past one of the workers from personnel and headed for the door. Once in the hallway, she noticed a security guard standing at attention.

Mark followed her out and instructed him, "Please see Ms. Tillman to her car. She is not to speak with anyone or take anything except her personal items."

CHAPTER 27

Batman walked into his room to find Nedra curled up fully clothed in his bed. He was still smarting from what had happened between him and her, and he and Lisa. The past week and a half had been spent quietly. Without speaking, he walked past her into the bathroom and shut the door. He took a face towel and washed his face with cold water. As he did, the door opened and Nedra stood there looking like death's twin sistah.

"Batman, I need to talk to you," she whispered.

The last time she had approached him with that soft posture, they had fought like cats and dogs. "No thanks, I'll just as well pass if it's alright with you."

He walked back into the bedroom and grabbed the remote. Nedra followed close behind and took it out of his hand. Using the same pathetic voice, she murmured, "No, Batman, we have to talk." Tears began to roll down her face. "If we don't talk, I think I'm going to kill myself."

The sincerity of her comments robbed him of his anger. He took the remote from her and tossed it to the side then took her hand and led her to the bed. Her tears melted whatever coldness he felt toward her. He pulled her close. "Nedra, what's going on?"

In spite of what had happened, Nedra wanted to appear strong. For years, she had been developing her tough professional female exterior, and even in the face of betrayal attempted to maintain it.

She lifted her head and wiped the tears from her eyes. "Batman, I got fired today, and I may be getting prosecuted tomorrow."

Nedra loved her job. It was trying, but she was committed to doing everything to help the patients who came into the clinic. Not only did she love her job, but she was good at it. She had moved from field worker to supervisor because she knew all the tricks and could locate and get people in better than anyone at the health department. She couldn't believe how stupid of a mistake she had made. The betrayal by Brian had led her to act and become someone she was incapable of being. Right then she wished she had never said to hell with God and everyone and had maintained her standards.

"Say what?" he replied incredulously.

"I got fired," she answered. "A girl came into the clinic, and she named Brian. She was HIV positive and I told him. He must have found her and beaten her up."

"A girl named Brain? She was positive? He beat her up? Nedra, what are you talking about?" Batman thought he must have sounded like that double-talking rooster from the cartoons, Foghorn Leghorn.

She shook her head to signal what he had repeated was what she'd said. Moreover, what he had heard was in fact true. His mind raced as fast as his heart. To him it was amazing how regular people could find themselves in so much drama.

He knew now was not the time to ask any details beyond what she had provided. Shifting gears, he began to search for how they could address the immediate problems of her being fired and the potential prosecution.

"Alright," he said, "what facts do they have on you? I mean, how do they know it was you? Couldn't Brian have found out from some-one else or on his own?"

Nedra looked up and shook her head no. "They've talked to the worker who handled the case, and now they're going to talk to Brian and the girl. I'm sure Brian will name me to save himself."

Of this Batman was sure. Brian would probably tell so fast he would get a nosebleed. "Look, let me do some checking. When do you have to go back and meet with them?"

"I'm not sure. They said they would contact me when they were ready."

"Good. First thing is we're not going to worry about this. The second thing is I used to work for the county. If I'm right, you're entitled to have a representative when you meet with them. It can be any-one of your choosing. It's normally a lawyer, but doesn't have to be. When they call you to meet, let me know and I'll see that you have the best representative for the job. In the mean time, I want you to get yourself together. I don't know about Brian, but I love you. I love you. I love you. I love you. And there's no way in the hell I'm about to let you go out like no punk."

He moved around to the other side of the bed and turned on the television. "Anything special?" he asked, motioning to the tube.

"No," she said.

"Good, then we'll watch Fred Sanford reruns."

Batman located the channel he was hoping to find and sat down the remote. No sooner had he gotten situated on the bed did a thought come to him. He looked at her and said, "Nedra, I need to know if you trust me? I mean if you really *really* trust me."

Nedra looked confused. He knew she trusted him, but needed to hear it from her. She smiled as he expected she would and replied sin-cerely, "Batman, of course I trust you. I don't always agree with you, but nevertheless I trust you."

"Good. Cause I'm going to ask you to do something."

He moved from the bed and went to the dresser. Once there, he pulled out the top middle drawer and turned it over. Attached under the bottom was a homemade package holder he had made using tape and an old envelope. Careful not to rip the envelope, he slid in two fingers and brought out what was left of a dime bag of red bud reefer. There were two jumbos already rolled. He took one, moved back to where he originally sat and fired it up.

It had been more than three weeks since he had last gotten high. He had resolved to stop smoking altogether, but right now he had bigger fish to fry. He inhaled deeply as Nedra watched. He could tell she was uncertain of just what was happening. He took another pull, held it in and handed the joint to her.

She looked at him suspiciously. "Batman, what are you doing? You know I don't smoke dope."

"Nedra, trust me. I know what I'm doing."

"I do trust you, but if you know what you're doing, then you may want to let me in on it."

Batman withdrew the joint and took another hit. He gave it time to move throughout his lungs then exhaled slowly. "You remember that movie we saw a long time ago called *Flash Gordon in the Twenty First Century?*"

Nedra nodded slightly, indicating that she vaguely remembered it.

"Well do you remember when they brought Flash up on all those charges of crimes against the universe?" he asked. "I'm not sure how many charges they had against him, but he had a little Martian lawyer who would rub his hand over his fist like this." Batman made the movement with his hands, resembling that of the character in the movie. "In fact his name was Hand-over-fist. Anyway, during the trial Flash became extremely nervous. All the while, Hand-over-fist kept saying, 'Don't worry, I've got an angle.' Well, Nedra, I'm going to tell you what Hand-over-fist told Flash. Don't worry 'cause Batman's got an angle. You just have to trust me."

He handed the joint back to her. This time she took it slowly and pulled on it. He signaled for her to do so, and she did it again.

"Deeper," he said, "take a real deep breath and let it go throughout your lungs."

CHAPTER 28

Nedra received the call Friday morning that she was to meet with her bosses and the representatives from personnel. After hanging up, she walked into Batman's bedroom. She looked slightly better than she had the previous day, but he could tell she was still upset. The dark rings under her eyes had thickened because of a lack of sleep.

She stood by the door and said, "That was them."

"Who?" he asked, wanting to know exactly who was leading the charge.

"The people from personnel. They said we have to meet with them Monday at ten."

"Did they say anything else?" he asked solemnly. "I need to know in detail everything that was said."

"Yeah, we talked some more. The guy was pretty nice. At least as nice as he could be considering the circumstances. He said they had completed the investigation. A police detective had interviewed Brian and Jackie. The way he sounded, I don't think we have much of a chance for saving my job. The best we can hope for is I don't go to jail."

She finished and hung her head in defeat. The tears started to flow again as she murmured, "I can't believe how big a fool I was. You tried to warn me, but I wouldn't listen. Now look at me. Lord what am I going to do if I have to go to jail?"

Batman sat up on the edge of the bed and spoke defiantly. "Nedra, now is not the time to cash in your chips. You said you trusted me, and for now you have to hold on to that."

"Did they say what Brian said?"

She weakly nodded yes, and he asked, "Did he mention anything about you all having sex?"

She wiped her face. "I don't think so. At least the man didn't say he did. They just said he admitted to beating up Jackie and that a disciplinary letter would be placed in his file."

Batman shook his head in disbelief. Brian had flipped like a pancake. On the promise that he would only receive a letter in his file, he had readily told that Nedra had given him the information. He prayed Brian hadn't mentioned the sexual affair. Batman surmised that Brian's failure to do so was not to protect Nedra, but in hopes of keeping his adulterous relationship out of the mix. The thought of Brian's deal strengthened Batman's resolve to make sure Nedra wasn't left holding the bag.

"Nedra, this is what I need for you to do. Go and call the guy you spoke with back. Tell him you spoke with your representative, and we can only meet at two. You got me? We can only meet at two. Also, tell him to expect a call from me."

Moving the meeting to two was a negotiating ploy on Batman's part. He wanted to take control, and the first way to do so was to arrange a time more amenable to them. He'd learned long ago that when negotiating, nothing was small or insignificant. He was tempted to try and have the meeting moved altogether, but felt this would be a deal breaker to the extent it could cause personnel to take a hard line.

Nedra left and returned ten minutes later, signaling she had done as he had instructed. Without waiting, Batman reached for the cordless she was holding and pressed redial. He covered the mouthpiece with one hand and asked, "Is this his direct line?"

She nodded "yes" as he waited for an answer. On the third ring, what he guessed was a white male picked up. "Good morning, personnel, Stan speaking, may I help you please?"

"Stan, Carter Osborne," he said as if they were old friends. "I'm Nedra Tillman's representative and was calling to get some information before the meeting on Monday."

Stan spoke cautiously, saying, "I spoke with Nedra and gave her as much information as I'm aware of. I'm not sure what else I can offer."

"Yes she told me the two of you spoke," Batman said as Nedra looked on. "First, I truly appreciate your keeping an open mind about this whole affair until we can meet and hopefully get it resolved. What she didn't say is who would be at the meeting. Could you give me an indication of who will be there?"

"Sure. I guess so," he answered, unsure of what harm it would cause. "Don't hold me to it, but I expect her supervisor, her supervisor's supervisor, me, a co-worker, a county attorney and a stenographer."

His mention of an attorney and stenographer caught Batman in the mid-section. He thought about the brother, Colin something, who shot up the subway in New York and chose to represent himself. In Batman's opinion, the man was mentally ill and the judge should never have allowed it. However, he did and was convicted and harshly sentenced. Subsequently, *Newsweek* ran an article with him on the front page. In a caption beneath his picture it read, "A Fool for a Client." Batman could see Nedra walking into that meeting with him serving as her advocate as being just that.

He was uncomfortable with this aspect. "Stan, I'm sorry, but if an attorney is going to be present, then we will have to cancel the meeting. I'm sure you understand."

There was no immediate reply to his comment. "Well when do you think we could do it?" Stan asked.

"Well the soonest we could probably meet would be another four weeks."

Now it was Stan's time to have the wind knocked out of him. Stumbling he replied, "Another four weeks. I'm sorry, but this matter can't wait that long."

Batman cut him off interjecting, "Yes, I agree. Please know we want this resolved as expeditiously as possible. But it will take at least one week to find an attorney who specializes in these type cases, and I can only guess three weeks for him to clear his calendar. However, we are more than glad to meet without either of our legal advocates being present."

Batman held the phone silently and waited for his reply. He was the furthest thing from an attorney and wasn't about to fool himself into walking into a trap.

"Well, I don't see any reason why we can't go on without one," Stan said. "Let's agree for now that no attorney will be present. I will call you and reschedule if anything changes."

Immediately following his conversation with Stan, Batman called Andrea Rivera at EEO. He understood that this was not a classic EEO case, but felt she was aware of personnel rules and regulations, which he could make use of to help Nedra. She had received the promotion for which she had arranged his new position and was more than happy to talk. After informing her of the situation, she provided what information she could but was pessimistic of a favorable outcome. He told her as he had told Nedra, "Don't worry, I have an angle."

She wished him well and made him promise to reveal his angle if it came through. If he knew her, she would probably use it the first chance she thought she could get something in return.

Monday morning came, and Batman woke up earlier than usual. He called in to let his crew know he would be taking the day off. He woke up Nedra and said, "Show time. Get ready because we need to be out of here in an hour."

"Why so early?" Nedra rolled over. "The meeting isn't until two."

"Don't worry, I've got an angle. But we have to be out of here in an hour. We have to go to the doctor."

"For what?" she asked suspiciously. "There's nothing wrong with me. Is there anything wrong with you?"

Batman walked over to the bed and pulled the covers off. She threw a pillow at him. He jumped out of the way laughing. "No, my dear, there's nothing wrong with me."

"Then why do we need to see a doctor?"

"Nedra, don't worry, I have an angle."

CHAPTER 29

Batman and Nedra arrived at the 401 Building at two-fifteen. Nedra was very worried about arriving late, but Batman had assured her they needed to take control. He'd learned during an organizational behavior class, the one semester he'd spent in school, people that are more powerful require less powerful people to wait for them. He wanted to send a message to her bosses that they weren't coming to beg and that they meant business. After entering the building, they took the elevator to the fourth floor and headed for the district personnel office.

They arrived at the fourth floor office to be greeted by Mark, his supervisor and the two personnel specialist who had attended the previous meeting. Batman and Nedra were escorted to a small conference room where everyone took their seats. Still on his power kick, Batman moved to the head of the table. Nedra and he had discussed seating positions prior to coming. She was to sit as far from him as possible. That way the reviewers would be forced to look back and forth rather than having the luxury of taking them both in at the same time.

Mark was the first to speak. "We all know why we're here, and we should get started. Nedra, as your supervisor I can say I'm sorry it's come to this. But we've concluded our investigation and have found that you knowingly broke confidentiality. Not only did you put the health department in legal jeopardy, but you risked the life of a young lady. I've spoken with the personnel specialists, and they've recommended that you be immediately fired and prosecuted."

The idea of being fired and prosecuted shook Nedra. They had agreed that whatever happened she was not to speak, and she was to appear calm. Batman wanted to give the impression she was innocent and thus deserving to keep her job. However, her nervousness showed through the disguise they had worked on.

It was now his turn to speak. Batman looked at Mark and moved his glance slowly around the room. He ensured each person knew he was taking them in and sizing them up. Speaking as though to friends, he said, "Mark, you said you've done a thorough investigation. Would you please explain how you could have accomplished that without talking with Nedra?"

Batman paused while Mark searched for an appropriate response but cut him off before he could offer it. "You talked to a rogue cop, and you talked to a young lady who'd been severely traumatized, but you've yet to talk to the one person who acted on behalf of the department."

Mark was at a loss for words. He had not expected to be the person under scrutiny. An investigation had taken place, but it had failed to include Nedra. He looked at the personnel specialist but got no support.

Mark turned to Nedra. "I don't see where that would matter. The evidence is overwhelming. However, if there is anything you'd like to say to help your situation, we are more than willing to listen."

All eyes turned to Nedra. She sat perfectly still, not saying a word. It was exactly as she and Batman had previously discussed. She had overcome the initial shock of hearing she would be prosecuted and was playing her role excellently. Batman gave them the opportunity to see she would not be shaken.

"I think this can all be worked out. As Nedra's representative, I believe I can provide the information to make sense of this. However, I need to speak with these gentlemen alone."

Batman looked at Mark and his supervisor, saying, "Could I ask that you gentlemen allow us a little time together privately."

Everyone was totally unprepared for his request. The faces in the room were aghast as well as bewildered. What he was about to do, he hadn't even shared with Nedra. Mark looked to the personnel specialists. They seemed unsure of whether his request was appropriate.

Before anyone could mount resistance, Batman said, "Please. I'm sure we would all like to get this resolved. Give me five minutes alone with these gentlemen, and we can probably head off making a huge mistake."

One of the personnel specialists broke the impasse. "I don't know what you have in mind, but I don't see a reason why we can't listen."

As he finished speaking, the other nodded his agreement. Mark and his supervisor moved for the door. Before they were out, Batman looked at Nedra and said, "Would you please leave also?" Nedra gave him a look to suggest she hadn't heard correctly. "Yes, you too please. I think what's about to be said should be said privately."

After everyone had exited, Batman shut the door. He opened his briefcase and pulled out the lab reports from Nedra and his morning visit. They had gone to the Haitian clinic on 79th and had waited for the results. He showed them to the two remaining gentleman and made his pitch. Fifteen minutes later, all three walked out of the conference room into the lobby where Nedra and the others were waiting. Smiling, Batman signaled to Nedra the meeting was over, shook hands with the men and said goodbye. Before he reached the door, he turned and again thanked each of them. There was no need to speak with Mark or his supervisor. He knew the generalist would fill in the gaps after they had spoken with their director.

Outside the building, Nedra couldn't wait for him to tell her what had happened. "You seemed pretty happy when you came out. I hope you didn't sell me down the river?"

Batman walked in stride as he took her hand and began to skip. "You're lucky I didn't have to. You're even luckier that I had an angle."

"I hear you," she said, "I just wish you'd let me in on it. Do I have my job or not?"

Batman stopped walking and looked at her. He did all he could to control the happiness inside without shouting it out. "Nedra, not only do you have your job, but you're getting six weeks of paid vacation."

Nedra's mouth fell open and she gasped. "I'm getting what?"

"Sweetheart, I just got you six weeks of paid vacation. That's forty two days, thirty working days, to do whatever you want."

Nedra grabbed him around the neck and gave him a big hug. She began jumping, shouting and screaming. It came to her that she was drawing a lot of attention from people passing by, and she calmed. She was about to give him another hug when she stopped and asked, "Batman, how the hell did we go in there with me about to be fired and sent to jail and walk out with my job and six weeks paid vacation?" She stopped and put her hands on her hips. Joy replaced with concern, Nedra asked, "Batman, what the hell did you tell those people when everyone left the room?"

"This morning when we went to the clinic I told you to take a urine test for diabetes."

She nodded her head and continued to listen.

"I said the reason was that stress affected body organs and if we were going to fight we needed to be in good health."

His telling her this had worked like a charm. It had really been a stroke of luck. He had banked on her natural cynicism being low and depended on her going along. Under normal circumstances, she would have certainly told him he was crazy. To his delight, she had submitted.

"I'm sorry," he said sincerely. "I wasn't completely honest. If I had been, you would have never gone along. The truth is that diabetes test you thought you took was actually a drug test for reefer." Batman started back toward the Gator and said innocently, "We needed a reason for you having broken confidentiality, so I told them that you were on drugs and needed rehabilitation."

Nedra stopped in mid-stride and shouted, "What! You told them what? Batman, I know you didn't tell those folks I was a drug addict, because if you did, I'm heading back right now and tell them the truth. There's no way I'm going back to work at that place with everyone thinking I'm a drug addict."

Batman pulled Nedra back to the corner. "Listen. I didn't have a choice. They had you dead to right. But the law says drug addiction is an illness. As such, a company can't fire you if you're ill. Especially if that illness is work related. I told them the stress of working around people dying of AIDS had pushed you to using. All you have to do is agree to rehabilitation. Hence, I told them about a six-week wellness program. I know just the one. It's over in Little Haiti. You don't even have to go. Just get the certificate and take it back. As far as anyone knowing, that's why I told everyone to leave. Your drug status cannot be shared. Not even with your bosses. If it is, then we'll sue for breach of confidentiality. It will go down as though you were ill, but for all they know it was knee surgery."

Nedra looked at him and a slow change came over her, her initial anger fading.

He decided to put the nail in the coffin. "Trust me. No one will ever know. Go back in six weeks and say you had knee surgery or that you needed the time off to attend to a sick family member. We can lay the ground work right now," he said closing the deal. "And guess what? You get to walk through the clinic and get your things as if nothing happened. I arranged for you to take some work home with you. When you finish, I can drop it back off at the clinic. The only thing is, at some point you will have to make it up to that worker. They said he was pretty disappointed in you."

Nedra smiled and punched him in the chest. Feigning pain, he bent over. "So that's how you repay me?"

"No. How I pay you is by taking you to dinner. But first let's go by the clinic and get Shag's results."

"I'm in," he said. "Just one thing though. Can I bring my friend?"

Nedra shook her head. "Back at it, huh? I see you and Lisa must have worked things out?"

CHAPTER 30

Nedra and Batman returned home from the clinic exhausted. The stress of the past few days had taken its toll on each of them. They retired to their rooms for a shower and nap. Waking, they dressed and headed for Shag's.

Shag must have seen them pull in because he was waiting with the door open when they walked up. His lightly decorated second floor apartment contained only the bare necessities.

"What's up, Kingfish? What's up, Nedra?" he asked as they entered.

Nedra and Batman greeted him and moved to the sofa. Nervous, he asked Nedra with a fake smile. "You have my results? Am I going to live or die?"

Nedra had her game face on and didn't bite. She spoke as she would to a patient, using Shag's real formal name. "Mr. Ellis, please have a seat."

Her response frightened Shag. He looked to Batman, but he had nothing to say. She had not shared Shag's results.

She continued, "Mr. Ellis, at this moment I am not your friend. You are a patient, and I am a counselor. Everything we talk about is confidential. Therefore, before we start I'm going to ask Mr. Osborne to step outside. Do you understand?"

Shag was at a loss for words. Batman didn't know what to make of the scene. Nedra looked at Batman and signaled he was to leave but wait outside. Following her cue, he stood and walked outside.

"Mr. Ellis, two weeks ago I preformed a HIV test on you," she said professionally. "The result of that test is back. The result is negative."

The news of the negative result was a relief to Shag. He wiped his forehead and sighed loudly. He moved to say something but Nedra continued, "Mr. Ellis, I need to inform you that because this test is negative, it does not mean that you are not infected. With HIV there is a window in which you may be infected, but the test came back negative. This is because the antibodies are not sufficiently high enough for detection by this test. In order to ensure you are negative, you must abstain from all risky behavior and be retested in four weeks. If that result comes back negative, then we can say with more certainty that you are not infected."

Shag had yet to speak. Nedra's approach had initially left him thinking he was positive. The news that he was negative was just beginning to resonate.

He regained his composure. "Can Batman come back now?"

Nedra nodded yes, and he called, "Batman."

Batman walked back to his seat beside Nedra. Shag looked at the both of them and said, "Hey guys, I'm sorry for the trouble."

"Shag, it was no trouble," Nedra said. "It's just we have to look out for ourselves. We're going to do what we're going to do, but we have to protect ourselves while we're doing it. God knows I love both of you and don't want anything to happen to either of you."

Batman looked at his watch to signal it was time to go. The whole scene combined with all the drama of the past week had pushed him into emotional overload. Standing, he commented, "If that's it, we'd best be leaving."

Nedra remained seated. "No, that's not it. There's one more thing. Before we go I'd like to pray."

Without thinking, Batman replied, "Pray about what?"

"About us."

Shag and Batman looked at each other. Batman was comfortable with his relationship with God and had no problem praying. Shag's look told him he wasn't about to object.

Batman broke the silence, saying, "Fire away."

They all stood and held hands. "Heavenly Father, we thank you for the blessings of this day," Nedra prayed. "We thank you for new mercies, and we thank you for your grace that is always sufficient. We thank you that you are ready, willing, and able to keep those things that we have committed unto you against that day. Father, right here and right now we commit our minds, bodies, and spirits unto you. We ask that you would protect and keep us from all hurt, harm and evil. We ask that you would protect us from ourselves and from the lusts of our flesh."

Nedra became silent and tightly squeezed Batman's hand. He opened his eyes and saw tears streaming down her face. He worked his hand free from hers and stepped closer to her. He pulled her close and used his free hand to place her head on his chest.

Sniffling, she continued, "Father, as we stand here, we ask that you forgive us for the people we have hurt. As we've asked for our-selves, we ask the same for Brian and his wife, Jackie, Lisa and whomever else we may have hurt. Amen."

Shag and Batman chimed in, "Amen," and they all came together for a three-person hug.

CHAPTER 31

Nedra and Batman arrived at Mike's Seafood Restaurant around seven and took their seats. The day had been filled with good news. She had gotten her job back and Shag's test had come back negative. He could only hope they would stay that way. *Mr. Pimp'em Hard had better be careful not to get pimped by the Big Ninja,* he thought. Prior to taking their seats, he had informed the waiter that his date would be joining them. He'd met her some weeks earlier at Big Daddy's. Since that time, they had conversed off and on. After his fiasco with Lisa, he decided to try a different approach. He looked up and saw the waiter approaching with her in tow.

As she arrived, he stood and said, "Nedra, I'd like to introduce you to Claire. Claire, meet Nedra."

He leaned over and took Claire's hand, pulled her to him and kissed her lightly on the cheek. She instinctively turned to receive the kiss and smiled as they both sat down.

Nedra looked at them in astonishment.

Batman noticed her facial expression and attempted to respond. However, before he could say anything, Nedra threw up her hands and said, "I know. It's rough on rats and tough on cats."

ABOUT THE AUTHOR

Chris Parker is a married father of two residing in the greater-Atlanta metropolitan area. Born in Mississippi, he attended and holds degrees from the University of MS (Ole Miss), Louisiana State University and Emory University. An avid outdoorsman, he spends his free time participating in and watching sports. He first began writing while in the Marine Corps and continues until this day.

Excerpt from

A RED POLKA DOT IN A WORLD FULL OF PLAID

BY

VARION JOHNSON

Release Date: November 2005

CHAPTER 1

"Why didn't you tell me?"

Mom was leaning over the sink, her hands submerged in soapy water. "Maxine, what are you talking about?"

I tightened my grip on the cordless phone. "You know exactly what I'm talking about!"

Her head snapped up. She spun around so fast, suds flew from her fingertips and splashed against my face. "How dare you use that tone of voice with–"

"My tone of voice?" I tried to stop myself from shaking. I didn't know whether to laugh or scream. Instead, I hurled the phone against the wall and watched its plastic pieces scatter across the linoleum.

"Girl, what the hell is your problem?" Mom screamed as she charged toward me.

"Why didn't you tell me my father was still alive?"

She froze. "What – what are you talking about?"

"Who do you think that last call was from?"

Wrinkles shot into my mother's mahogany-colored skin. Suddenly she looked a lot older than her forty-two years. "He called?"

"I see you're not denying it now." I turned and began to march out.

"Maxine Edrice Phillips, don't even *think* about walking out of this room."

I jerked to a stop. As much as I hated to admit it, Mom's voice always had a certain power over me. It was like a leash, yanking me back to reality.

"Let me explain," she said, in a softer voice.

I crossed my arms. "Yeah Mom, please explain how in eighteen years, you couldn't find the time to tell me he was alive."

"I was only trying to protect you."

"Protect me? Don't I have the right to know who my father is?"

She frowned. "Don't raise your voice at me."

"The hell with my voice—"

Her hand was across my face before I could finish my statement. The slap was cold and quick, and so strong I almost lost my balance.

A quiet iciness settled around us. Mom stared at me, in the loudest silence I had ever experienced. Her hand lingered in the air as if she was going to hit me again. Her eyes were so intense, I couldn't bear to look at them.

For the first time ever, I felt uncomfortable around my mother. Of course, maybe she wasn't my mother after all. My mother would never lie to me or slap me.

I couldn't take the silence any longer. I stormed toward the door.

"Where are you going?" she yelled after me.

I didn't bother to turn around. "Out!"

A cool summer breeze struck my hot cheek as I headed toward my magic carpet on wheels, a lime green hatchback Hyundai. I started the car and tried to ignore Mom's gaze as she stood in the doorway.

I could still feel her eyes on me, as I pulled out of the driveway and sped down the street.

Deke's mother opened the door and stared at me. I hated to imagine how I looked. I could feel my cherry-brown, frizzled hair pointing in all directions. In my too old, too baggy sweats, I probably looked like Medusa in an aerobics video.

"Maxine, come in," she said as she ushered me inside. Suitcases and bags were scattered across the den. Deke's stepfather was in the process of trying to force one of the suitcases to close. He looked up as I entered the room.

"Maxine," he said. "How much do you weigh?"

"What?"

"Never mind, just come over here and sit on this suitcase."

Great – not only was I ugly and crazy, but I was also fat.

"Jason, will you leave Maxine alone? I'm sure she didn't come here to help you pack." Deke's mother wrapped her arm around my shoulder and gave me a small squeeze. "Deke is in his room."

I left Mr. Ashland struggling with the zipper and walked down the hallway to Deke's room. I could hear him mumbling from behind the door. I tried to press down my hair before knocking.

Immediately the talking stopped and he opened the door. Deke's frame took up most of the doorway. His dark, chocolate skin was like the photo negative of my own khaki-toned complexion. Deke always joked about me being the only girl that reminded him of a pair of pants.

A seemingly concerned frown came to his face. He pressed his lips together and looked me up and down, like he was checking to make sure I was okay. His gaze hovered at my face, on my cheek.

I shrugged.

He nodded as if he understood everything, and let me into the room.

I pushed the pillows off his bed and collapsed onto the marshmallow mattress. "You won't believe the day I've had."

He held his finger up. "Hold on for a second," he said. He picked up the phone receiver lying on his desk. "Yvonne, can I call you back?" A frown came to his face. "Yes, it's her." Another pause. "What do you mean, don't bother calling you back?" By now, I could hear yelling on the other end of the phone. "Of course you're as important to me as – Hello?"

Deke sighed and hung up the phone. "What were you saying?"

"Listen, I can come back later–"

"She'll get over it," he said as he dropped beside me on the bed. "Tell me what happened."

Good old Deke. Just sitting next to him made me feel calmer. He was the closest thing I had to a best friend; probably the closest thing I had to a friend at all.

It had been almost thirteen years since I first met Deke. Mom and I had recently moved from New York to Columbia, South Carolina. I remembered being dragged to my new kindergarten class in an ugly pink dress I didn't want to wear. As the teacher announced my name and as I walked to my seat, all the other kids laughed and pointed at me. I was pale and awkward, with a funny-shaped head, rust-colored hair, and that abominable pink dress didn't help. Later that day, I saw Deke reading a book in the corner. He looked over at me and frowned as if he didn't know what I was. Finally he came over and handed me a book. We had been inseparable ever since.

I looked at Deke. "My father is alive."

His mouth dropped open. At least I wasn't the only one surprised.

"Are you sure?"

I nodded.

"What do you know about him?"

"Nothing much," I said. "Just that he and Mom split up when I was about a year old."

Deke became quiet, and I knew he was thinking about his father. Not Jason Ashland, the man who raised him, but his biological father – the man who ran out on Deke and his mother years ago.

"I wish I knew why he left," I said. "I mean, I'm sure there's a good reason." I ignored the grimace on Deke's face. "Anyway, he's pretty much stayed out of our lives until now. He would sometimes call every few years, but that was about it. But a few weeks ago, he called Mom and said that he wanted to meet me."

"After all this time?"

I nodded. "Mom didn't think it was a good idea, so he decided to call me himself. Unfortunately, I hung up on him before we could really talk about anything."

"Why did you hang up on him?"

"I was nervous. I didn't know what to say, what to think, or what to do. I didn't even believe he was telling the truth until I confronted Mom."

Deke paced the small room. "You know, your mother called for you. She told me about the...altercation y'all had." He picked up the phone. "You have to call her."

"I don't *have* to do anything." I fought the temptation to rub my tender cheek. "Are your parents ready for their trip?" I asked.

He nodded. "Beginning tomorrow night, I'll have two whole weeks to myself."

"You mean, you and Yvonne will have two whole weeks to yourselves," I said with a smirk.

"Nope. I'm taking a break from everyone, including her."

I smiled. For any ordinary eighteen-year-old, two weeks without any parental supervision would be an everyday prom night, without the dinner and fancy dresses. But knowing Deke, he would spend the entire time watching cartoons and eating cereal.

"Stop trying to change the subject." He still had the phone in his hand. "Are you going to talk to your mother?"

"She slapped me, Deke. Am I supposed to forget that?"

He sighed, and his voice grew quiet. "Maybe you deserved it."

I jumped from the bed and got in his face. "I know you didn't say that."

He took a step back. "Maxine, she's your mother. She deserves a certain amount of respect."

I pouted, but I knew he was right. I had never cursed at my mother before. I never had any reason to, until today.

Wait a minute. She was the one who hit me. Why did I feel guilty? I finally rubbed my cheek. She must have knocked something loose with that slap.

Again he extended the phone to me. "Call her."

I shook my head. What did he want me to do, thank her for slapping me?

"Didn't you and Yvonne break up a couple of weeks ago?" I glanced around the room for pictures of her, but there were none. There was one of Deke and his family, and one of me. That was it.

"I see there's no point in arguing with you." Deke dropped the phone back on his desk. "Yeah, we broke up, but we got back together."

"You know what your problem is?" I didn't wait for a response. "You need to have sex."

Deke frowned. "You know I can't do that."

"Why not? It's not hard to do. Just get naked and–"

"I don't need lessons." He picked up the two pillows I had pushed to the floor and returned them to the bed. "Anyway, at least I have a girlfriend. I don't see any guys beating down your door."

Good point.

"No guy in his right mind would ask me out. I mean, look at me. I'm a skinny black girl with gray eyes and hair that has a mind of its own."

My skin tone was what some people called "high yellow." My hair had been a bane my entire life, always pointing every which way except the way I wanted. It constantly changed colors during the year, from an almost respectable reddish-brown hue in the winter to an embarrassing strawberry-red, burnt-orange, cherry-brown mix in the summer. Deke would try to make me feel better by describing me as "exotic." I just considered myself a freak of nature.

"Why are you so hard on yourself?" Deke asked. "You're very pretty."

Yeah, easy for him to say. Deke had the physique of an overpaid pro-football player. Half the girls in town had a crush on him. The other half was either blind, stupid, or insane. I included myself in the insane category.

"So when are you going to talk to your mother?"

I smirked. "The day after never?"

"You have to go home eventually."

I ran my fingers through Deke's thick, curly hair and leaned close to his ear. "I figured you and I would just run off, shack up, and have a couple of illegitimate children."

Deke crossed his arms.

"Or, maybe not."

It was almost midnight by the time I returned home. I gently unlocked the back door and crept into the house. I hoped Mom was asleep, because the last thing I needed was to get into another argument with her. I was doing fine until the floor squeaked underneath me.

"Maxine, is that you?"

Mom appeared from her room and walked down the hallway. Katherine Phillips was, by far, the most beautiful woman I knew. Where I stood awkwardly, she stood gracefully. Where I stuttered, she sang. Her eyes were a soft hazel, not a hard gray, and her jet black hair looked like it was spun of silk. Her smooth, brown skin shimmered in the artificial light of the kitchen.

"I see you're finally home," she said. "I was worried about you."

"I'll bet."

Mom seemed to ignore my comment. She pulled out a chair from the table and sat. "The way you ran out of the house, I–"

"Don't you understand? I don't want to talk to you."

Mom's face became long. "You probably think I'm the most evil person in the world, but believe me when I say my intentions were good."

"So lying is okay now. I knew those Ten Commandments weren't all they were cracked up to be."

"Maxine, you can't possibly understand–"

"No, I understand. You were so wrapped up in your feelings, you couldn't bother to tell me that my father was alive and that he wanted to meet me," I said. "And when I did ask about him, you slapped me. I think that's about all I can stomach for tonight."

Before she could respond, I ran into my room and slammed the door shut. In my mind, I could still see Mom sitting at the table with that same expression on her face. I thought yelling at her would make me feel better. I was mistaken.

I looked in the mirror. There was still the slightest hint of redness to my face. One of the downfalls of having light skin was that it bruised extremely easily.

I heard a chair scrape along the kitchen floor and footsteps travel down the hallway. They stopped in front of my room.

I walked back to my door and placed my trembling hand on the knob. I was unsure whether I should open it or leave it closed. I listened. Finally, the footsteps moved away. After a few more moments of silence, I opened the door. All that remained in the hallway was a small note. It had Jack Phillips's name on it. And his number.

As I picked the note up and walked back to my bed, I couldn't help staring at the faded slip of paper. After taking a few deep breaths, I picked up the phone. I hurriedly dialed the number, before I lost my nerve.

The phone rang.

What if I'm making a mistake? He could be asleep. Or what if he's married and I wake up his wife? Or what if—

"Hello, this is Jack."

I paused, trying to force the words out of my mouth.

"Hello?" the voice said on the other end of the phone. "Is anyone there?"

"Um...hi," I stammered. "This is Maxine Phillips, your daughter."

ROUGH ON RATS AND TOUGH ON CATS

2005 Publication Schedule

January

A Heart's Awakening
Veronica Parker
$9.95
1-58571-143-8

Falling
Natalie Dunbar
$9.95
1-58571-121-7

February

Echoes of Yesterday
Beverly Clark
$9.95
1-58571-131-4

A Love of Her Own
Cheris F. Hodges
$9.95
1-58571-136-5

Higher Ground
Leah Latimer
$19.95
1-58571-157-8

March

Misconceptions
Pamela Leigh Starr
$9.95
1-58571-117-9

I'll Paint a Sun
A.J. Garrotto
$9.95
1-58571-165-9

Peace Be Still
Colette Haywood
$12.95
1-58571-129-2

April

Intentional Mistakes
Michele Sudler
$9.95
1-58571-152-7

Conquering Dr. Wexler's Heart
Kimberley White
$9.95
1-58571-126-8

Song in the Park
Martin Brant
$15.95
1-58571-125-X

May

The Color Line
Lizzette Grayson Carter
$9.95
1-58571-163-2

Unconditional
A.C. Arthur
$9.95
1-58571-142-X

Last Train to Memphis
Elsa Cook
$12.95
1-58571-146-2

June

Angel's Paradise
Janice Angelique
$9.95
1-58571-107-1

Suddenly You
Crystal Hubbard
$9.95
1-58571-158-6

Matters of Life and
   Death
Lesego Malepe, Ph.D.
$15.95
1-58571-124-1

2005 Publication Schedule (continued)

July

Class Reunion
Irma Jenkins/John
  Brown
$12.95
1-58571-123-3

Wild Ravens
Altonya Washington
$9.95
1-58571-164-0

August

Path of Thorns
Annetta P. Lee
$9.95
1-58571-145-4

Timeless Devotion
Bella McFarland
$9.95
1-58571-148-9

Life Is Never As It Seems
J.J. Michael
$12.95
1-58571-153-5

September

Beyond the Rapture
Beverly Clark
$9.95
1-58571-131-4

Blood Lust
J. M. Jeffries
$9.95
1-58571-138-1

Rough on Rats and
  Tough on Cats
Chris Parker
$12.95
1-58571-154-3

October

A Will to Love
Angie Daniels
$9.95
1-58571-141-1

Taken by You
Dorothy Elizabeth Love
$9.95
1-58571-162-4

Soul Eyes
Wayne L. Wilson
$12.95
1-58571-147-0

November

A Drummer's Beat to
  Mend
Kay Swanson
$9.95

Sweet Reprecussions
Kimberley White
$9.95
1-58571-159-4

Red Polka Dot in a
  Worldof Plaid
Varian Johnson
$12.95
1-58571-140-3

December

Hand in Glove
Andrea Jackson
$9.95
1-58571-166-7

Blaze
Barbara Keaton
$9.95

Across
Carol Payne
$12.95
1-58571-149-7

ROUGH ON RATS AND TOUGH ON CATS

Other Genesis Press, Inc. Titles

Acquisitions	Kimberley White	$8.95
A Dangerous Deception	J.M. Jeffries	$8.95
A Dangerous Love	J.M. Jeffries	$8.95
A Dangerous Obsession	J.M. Jeffries	$8.95
After the Vows	Leslie Esdaile	$10.95
(Summer Anthology)	T.T. Henderson	
	Jacqueline Thomas	
Again My Love	Kayla Perrin	$10.95
Against the Wind	Gwynne Forster	$8.95
A Lark on the Wing	Phyliss Hamilton	$8.95
A Lighter Shade of Brown	Vicki Andrews	$8.95
All I Ask	Barbara Keaton	$8.95
A Love to Cherish	Beverly Clark	$8.95
Ambrosia	T.T. Henderson	$8.95
And Then Came You	Dorothy Elizabeth Love	$8.95
Angel's Paradise	Janice Angelique	$8.95
A Risk of Rain	Dar Tomlinson	$8.95
At Last	Lisa G. Riley	$8.95
Best of Friends	Natalie Dunbar	$8.95
Bound by Love	Beverly Clark	$8.95
Breeze	Robin Hampton Allen	$10.95
Brown Sugar Diaries &	Delores Bundy &	$10.95
Other Sexy Tales	Cole Riley	
By Design	Barbara Keaton	$8.95
Cajun Heat	Charlene Berry	$8.95
Careless Whispers	Rochelle Alers	$8.95
Caught in a Trap	Andre Michelle	$8.95
Chances	Pamela Leigh Starr	$8.95
Dark Embrace	Crystal Wilson Harris	$8.95
Dark Storm Rising	Chinelu Moore	$10.95
Designer Passion	Dar Tomlinson	$8.95
Ebony Butterfly II	Delilah Dawson	$14.95

Erotic Anthology	Assorted	$8.95
Eve's Prescription	Edwina Martin Arnold	$8.95
Everlastin' Love	Gay G. Gunn	$8.95
Fate	Pamela Leigh Starr	$8.95
Forbidden Quest	Dar Tomlinson	$10.95
Fragment in the Sand	Annetta P. Lee	$8.95
From the Ashes	Kathleen Suzanne	$8.95
	Jeanne Sumerix	
Gentle Yearning	Rochelle Alers	$10.95
Glory of Love	Sinclair LeBeau	$10.95
Hart & Soul	Angie Daniels	$8.95
Heartbeat	Stephanie Bedwell-Grime	$8.95
I'll Be Your Shelter	Giselle Carmichael	$8.95
Illusions	Pamela Leigh Starr	$8.95
Indiscretions	Donna Hill	$8.95
Interlude	Donna Hill	$8.95
Intimate Intentions	Angie Daniels	$8.95
Just an Affair	Eugenia O'Neal	$8.95
Kiss or Keep	Debra Phillips	$8.95
Love Always	Mildred E. Riley	$10.95
Love Unveiled	Gloria Greene	$10.95
Love's Deception	Charlene Berry	$10.95
Mae's Promise	Melody Walcott	$8.95
Meant to Be	Jeanne Sumerix	$8.95
Midnight Clear	Leslie Esdaile	$10.95
(Anthology)	Gwynne Forster	
	Carmen Green	
	Monica Jackson	
Midnight Magic	Gwynne Forster	$8.95
Midnight Peril	Vicki Andrews	$10.95
My Buffalo Soldier	Barbara B. K. Reeves	$8.95
Naked Soul	Gwynne Forster	$8.95
No Regrets	Mildred E. Riley	$8.95
Nowhere to Run	Gay G. Gunn	$10.95

Object of His Desire	A. C. Arthur	$8.95
One Day at a Time	Bella McFarland	$8.95
Passion	T.T. Henderson	$10.95
Past Promises	Jahmel West	$8.95
Path of Fire	T.T. Henderson	$8.95
Picture Perfect	Reon Carter	$8.95
Pride & Joi	Gay G. Gunn	$8.95
Quiet Storm	Donna Hill	$8.95
Reckless Surrender	Rochelle Alers	$8.95
Rendezvous with Fate	Jeanne Sumerix	$8.95
Revelations	Cheris F. Hodges	$8.95
Rivers of the Soul	Leslie Esdaile	$8.95
Rooms of the Heart	Donna Hill	$8.95
Shades of Brown	Denise Becker	$8.95
Shades of Desire	Monica White	$8.95
Sin	Crystal Rhodes	$8.95
So Amazing	Sinclair LeBeau	$8.95
Somebody's Someone	Sinclair LeBeau	$8.95
Someone to Love	Alicia Wiggins	$8.95
Soul to Soul	Donna Hill	$8.95
Still Waters Run Deep	Leslie Esdaile	$8.95
Subtle Secrets	Wanda Y. Thomas	$8.95
Sweet Tomorrows	Kimberly White	$8.95
The Color of Trouble	Dyanne Davis	$8.95
The Price of Love	Sinclair LeBeau	$8.95
The Reluctant Captive	Joyce Jackson	$8.95
The Missing Link	Charlyne Dickerson	$8.95
Three Wishes	Seressia Glass	$8.95
Tomorrow's Promise	Leslie Esdaile	$8.95
Truly Inseperable	Wanda Y. Thomas	$8.95
Twist of Fate	Beverly Clark	$8.95
Unbreak My Heart	Dar Tomlinson	$8.95
Unconditional Love	Alicia Wiggins	$8.95
When Dreams A Float	Dorothy Elizabeth Love	$8.95

Whispers in the Night	Dorothy Elizabeth Love	$8.95
Whispers in the Sand	LaFlorya Gauthier	$10.95
Yesterday is Gone	Beverly Clark	$8.95
Yesterday's Dreams, Tomorrow's Promises	Reon Laudat	$8.95
Your Precious Love	Sinclair LeBeau	$8.95

Order Form

Mail to: Genesis Press, Inc.
P.O. Box 101
Columbus, MS 39703

Name _____

Address _____

City/State _____ Zip _____

Telephone _____

Ship to (if different from above)

Name _____

Address _____

City/State _____ Zip _____

Telephone _____

Credit Card Information

Credit Card # _____ ☐ Visa   ☐ Mastercard

Expiration Date (mm/yy) _____ ☐ AmEx   ☐ Discover

Qty.	Author	Title	Price	Total

Use this order form, or call 1-888-INDIGO-1	**Total for books** _____ **Shipping and handling:** $5 first two books, $1 each additional book _____ **Total S & H** _____ **Total amount enclosed** _____ *Mississippi residents add 7% sales tax*

Order Form

Mail to: Genesis Press, Inc.
P.O. Box 101
Columbus, MS 39703

Name _____
Address _____
City/State _____ Zip _____
Telephone _____

Ship to (if different from above)
Name _____
Address _____
City/State _____ Zip _____
Telephone _____

Credit Card Information
Credit Card # _____ ☐ Visa ☐ Mastercard
Expiration Date (mm/yy) _____ ☐ AmEx ☐ Discover

Qty.	Author	Title	Price	Total

Use this order form, or call 1-888-INDIGO-1	**Total for books** _____
	Shipping and handling:
	  $5 first two books,
	  $1 each additional book _____
	Total S & H _____
	Total amount enclosed _____

Mississippi residents add 7% sales tax

Order Form

Mail to: Genesis Press, Inc.
P.O. Box 101
Columbus, MS 39703

Name _____

Address _____

City/State _____ Zip _____

Telephone _____

Ship to (if different from above)

Name _____

Address _____

City/State _____ Zip _____

Telephone _____

Credit Card Information

Credit Card # _____ ☐ Visa ☐ Mastercard

Expiration Date (mm/yy) _____ ☐ AmEx ☐ Discover

Qty.	Author	Title	Price	Total

Use this order

form, or call

1-888-INDIGO-1

Total for books _____

Shipping and handling:
  $5 first two books,
  $1 each additional book _____

Total S & H _____

Total amount enclosed _____

Mississippi residents add 7% sales tax